TERRY W. BURNS
BEYOND THE SMOKE

journeyforth®

Greenville, South Carolina

Library of Congress Cataloging-in Publication Data
Burns, Terry, 1942-
   Beyond the smoke / Terry W. Burns.
      p. cm.
   Summary: When his parents are killed by Comanche raiders, sixteen-year-old
Bryan sets out to create a new life for himself in the western wilderness.
   ISBN 978-1-59166-929-6 (perfect bound pbk. : alk. paper)
   [1. Frontier and pioneer life—Fiction. 2. Orphans—Fiction. 3. Christian life—
Fiction.]   I. Title.
   PZ7.B93746Be 2008
   [Fic] —dc22
2008029361

Cover photo (cowboy): Craig Oesterling
Cover photos: www.istockphoto.com: Peter Zelei (background), Ivan Cholakov
(smoke), David T. Gomez (fence), Randy Plett (old paper)

Design by Nathan Hutcheon
Page layout by Michael Boone

© 2009 BJU Press
Greenville, South Carolina 29609
JourneyForth Books is a division of BJU Press.

Printed in the United States of America

ISBN 978-1-59166-929-6

15   14   13   12   11   10   9   8   7   6   5   4   3   2

Dedication

I promised my father-in-law, A. E. Pennington that I would dedicate my next book to him. He went to be with the Lord this past year and I offer this dedication in grateful thanks for his love and friendship. He gave me the most precious thing he had, one of his three daughters.

At the Northeast Texas Writers Group conference, Janet Mackey bought the right in a benefit auction to have a character named for her husband, Scott, in this book. The characters Janet and Scott are simply named for them and any actual resemblance to them or any other person is purely coincidental.

CONTENTS

1

Smoke arose in the distance.

Bryan Wheeler shaded his eyes as he stared at it. Something was not right, but there was no cause for concern.

Not yet.

He headed back that direction, saw tracks and knelt, fingered the tiny tracks, read them as an eastern boy would read a book. A rabbit for the pot.

At sixteen Bryan was already an accomplished hunter. His frame bordered on husky, solid, and well muscled. His sandy blonde hair and green eyes worked with his ready grin to tell everyone at a glance that he was always ready to have fun.

Cowboys his age were common on western ranches as were young soldiers riding with the cavalry or the Pony Express. Girls even younger got married and started families. On the frontier young people grew up fast . . . or they didn't grow up at all.

While his father handled the team or drove the wagon in the Oregon-bound wagon train, Bryan was expected to walk out and put meat on the table. It wasn't a new thing. Back in Missouri he handled this chore while his father worked the fields, beginning when he was barely big enough to keep the muzzle of the big weapon out of the dirt.

His dad would give him half a dozen bullets and expect an accounting for each and every one—something for the pot or a reason why a round was wasted. It was the way of the poor farmer. Scarce resources were not squandered.

Bryan stood and went in the direction of the tracks. Unable to see the ground he scanned the tall grass for the tiniest evidence of movement. He moved slowly, bringing his foot down toe first, Indian style, to minimize noise. Spotting some movement, he took a line to head it off, then waited until the rabbit scurried across a small clearing.

The animal was in the open only a moment . . . but it was enough.

The shot came quick and clean. He scooped the rabbit up by the ears and smiled. *A nice fat one! It'll make a good stew,* he thought.

He shaded his eyes to look off into the distance, wondered where the train was now. He knew it didn't move very fast, but certainly could eat up ground while a guy's attention was elsewhere. He was still puzzled by the smoke on the horizon. It was early to stop to cook.

He pushed it from his mind again. The wagon boss had probably found a really good campsite and decided to take advantage of it. That meant he had better hurry back with the rabbit, particularly if his mama already had the pot on.

He swung the rabbit in his left hand in order to keep his rifle at the ready in his right. As he moved out, his eyes constantly played across the ground to either side of his path. He wouldn't say no to a little more meat to fatten that stew.

A short time later Bryan glanced back to check his direction. *Hmm,* he thought, *the fires don't seem to be grouped tightly the way they should be with the train in a circle for the night. They seem to be in a straight line, spread out. That's strange!*

He immediately gave up hunting to step out quickly. As the worry came, he put a hand to his chest, a new tightness there. He had difficulty swallowing, his mouth unexpectedly dry.

He reached the top of the rise and his concerns proved to be justified. Bryan caught his breath as he looked down on the train. The smoke wasn't from cook fires, but from the smoldering ruins of several burned out wagons. Bodies lay everywhere.

He couldn't help himself; he began to cry. It wasn't the manly thing to do, but he didn't feel very manly right now.

Bryan entered camp warily, rifle at the ready. He tried to not look at the bodies, but couldn't help himself there either. Any other time it would have sickened him, but now it didn't seem real. He moved as if in a dream, his head swimming. The bright splotches of red were everywhere as if splashed by a demented painter. The air was tainted with a sickly sweet smell, but he scarcely noticed it.

He made straight for his parents' wagon, not wanting to see what he'd find there, but knowing he had to do it. He had to know.

Suddenly he stopped short. There they were . . . dead . . . no one alive in this whole train. He was alone. Bryan sat down hard on a stump, averting his eyes, staring off into space.

He had often been alone before. Alone hunting, alone for a walk, valued time off by himself. But it had always been a temporary thing, an enjoyable respite. This time he was ALONE! And he didn't know what to do.

Bryan didn't know how long he had sat there . . . or why, but at last some tiny part of the back of his brain began to nag at him. *What if the raiders come back?*

The thought chilled him like a blue norther. It shocked him back to reality. *Whatever I do, I can't just sit here.*

His first thought was to bury them, of course. But then, he was just a boy, how much could he do?

I could dig . . . what? One or two graves at most. I can't bury them all. And if the savages do come back and find fresh graves, they'd know somebody was alive and come after me.

It was a shock for him to realize he couldn't bury anybody.

Oh my! I have to go, and I have to go now, but where? And how? I wish it didn't have to be on foot, but there ain't any horses left. *Reckon that was the main thing they were after. I know, first I have to see what I can find that might help me survive.*

From their wagon he got his mother's Bible, some pictures, and a couple of changes of clothes. His father's handgun and rifle were gone. He knew the raiders had wanted guns and ammunition as badly as the horses. He took a little food and a pot big enough to cook in, but light enough to carry.

Then he steeled himself to do the hardest thing of all, he searched his father's body. He searched for the money he knew his father carried and the pocket watch that had belonged to his grandfather. He could scarcely see through the tears, apologized the whole time, but he knew he'd need that money . . . and he surely wanted the watch.

The money caused him to think. He knew there would be more money, but it also meant he would have to do the search all over again on other people. The rest wouldn't be as hard, but still mighty tough.

He felt like a sneak thief going from wagon to wagon searching for things he could use. He knew if any of these people could talk, they'd tell him he had to do it, but it didn't help. He still couldn't get over the feeling.

To make up for it, he gathered all of the letters and information he could find. He decided he would write each of their relations. They would want to know what happened, and he felt he owed it to them.

Suddenly he straightened up to look across the camp. *Old Abe used to carry a little hideout gun tucked in his belt in the back.* Bryan ran over to him and rolled him over. There it was, a little 32-caliber pocket gun, and it was loaded. *Where are his saddlebags?*

Finding them, Bryan took the old clothes out and wrapped inside them found a partial box of shells for the little gun, some beef jerky, and a small coffee pot with a parcel of coffee.

He could use the saddlebags to gather his gear in. He continued to search, particularly for blankets, but they seemed to have been prized by the raiders as well.

Ahh . . . here's a couple of old ones, but they look good to me.

He found and filled a canteen from a water barrel, then sat on the tailgate of a wagon to pack the things he'd found. It included a surprising amount of money, but he wouldn't stop to count it now. He was starting to feel the need to get out of there.

Reckon a Comanche ain't got no use for cash.

He'd heard the wagon boss comment about Comanche sign and felt pretty sure that was who had made the attack. There were no raiders left, so the attack had either been alarmingly successful, or they had carried off their dead.

He found a cash box in the Jorgenson wagon that had a sizable sum. He had known where they kept it. The box was too bulky, so he discarded it and put the money in his blanket roll. Bryan stood up. It seemed all he could do, and he had all the help these people had to give.

I'd like to hug my family goodbye, he thought, but couldn't bring himself to do it, not the way they looked. *This is not my family any more. I know that. They've gone on . . . gone to a better world.*

He got out his mother's Bible to read over them—over the entire train.

I owe them that much at least.

He opened the Bible, a familiar task as he had learned to read from its pages, read it each night before going to bed. Still, he was unsure where to turn, where would he find the verses he needed? The parson that was with them had read over graves on the trip. But he used a little book that was for weddings and funerals.

Bryan shook his head, he didn't have time to go look for that book. He knew comfort was in the Bible and felt ashamed that he didn't know where it was. He closed his eyes and asked for help. It was a brief, but heartfelt, earnest prayer. He opened the back cover of the Bible without looking.

He looked down, blinking to clear his vision, his eye settled on 2 Corinthians, chapter five. His mother had a passage underlined, verse 8, and he read it aloud, "We are confident, I say, and willing rather to be absent with the body, and to be present with the Lord."

Yes, he thought, *they aren't here any more. They are already with God.*

She had a notation written in the margin referencing John 14. He turned to it, and again found underlining at verse 26 and 27. Again he read aloud, "But the Comforter, which is the Holy Ghost, whom the Father will send in my name, he shall teach you all things, and bring all things to your remembrance, whatsoever I have said unto you. Peace I leave with you, my peace I give unto you: not as the world giveth, give I unto you. Let not your heart be troubled, neither let it be afraid."

He had read that before, but never had it spoken to his heart as it did now. Funny how you could read something in the Bible many times but find new meaning in it when your needs were different. He smiled. It was if the finger of his mother had pointed to these verses, as if she had told him they were all right and told him the Comforter would now be with him. The sadness was still a heavy weight on his chest, but he didn't feel as alone.

Then with tears again streaming down his face he closed the Bible, tucked it into his saddlebags, and said his last goodbye.

Bryan turned and looked out over the empty prairie. *I don't know what's out there . . . who is out there . . . and I don't know which way to go. My first decision as a man on my own, and I don't have the slightest idea of a direction to take.*

He voiced his concern out loud, "I have to find someplace that's safe before they return and find me. I need some kind of cover, and I need it mighty bad." He wiped his tear-stained face.

"But right now, I'd settle for sundown."

2

Bryan's head didn't seem to work right. It felt as if it were stuffed with cotton. The road swam in front of him, and he had difficulty walking straight. He couldn't remember ever being so confused. Wrestling out the simplest decision seemed to take all the concentration he could muster.

He looked at the lowering sun. His papa had told him if he held his arm at full length, the sun would move a hand span every hour, and he could measure time that way. His pa's hand was a lot bigger than Bryan's, but his arm was longer, too, so it was supposed to work out right.

Bryan measured the distance between the fiery ball and the horizon. He calculated he had a bit over two hours to get somewhere before it got dark. But where? He knew nothing about this country.

No ... wait ... that's not true. I know every inch of the ground we've covered so far. I covered it on foot hunting or walking by the wagon. Sure, that's it. Go the way I know. Go back.

Something about that didn't feel right. They'd been so focused on getting to Oregon that nothing was allowed to get in their way. It seemed to Bryan as if he would be letting them down if he turned back, but even at that, he knew it to be the smart play. He knew it had to be done.

Bryan turned and looked down the deep ruts leading off to the horizon. He remembered a good stand of rocks a ways back.

If I really get after it, I could make those rocks by dark.

He slung the blanket roll on his back, put the saddlebags and the canteen over his shoulders, hefted the rifle, and headed out at a brisk pace.

He nearly made it by dark, but had to pretty much feel his way along the last half hour. Finally the dark shapes loomed ahead of Bryan like a silent friend. He felt his way to them to find a place deep inside out of the wind where a fire wouldn't show. He gathered what firewood he could find and settled in.

The rabbit! I forgot the rabbit.

He settled for some of Abe's jerky and put some coffee on to cook on a double handful of fire. He'd done this before, had often camped out away from the train, sometimes by himself, sometimes with one of the other boys. When he did it then, it had been an adventure. Now it was . . . well . . . lonesome . . . more than that, terrifying.

The morning of a new day. Bryan always loved to see the sun come up, looked forward to what the day would bring. But today was different. His grief had settled into a physical thing. His chest ached, and there was a knot in the pit of his stomach. His head felt fuzzy and he was scared.

Yeah, I admit it. I'm really scared. I'm not old enough to be on my own like this. I thought I was near grown, but I was wrong, I'm just a kid. What in the world am I going to do?

He could hear his papa's voice. *When you have a big problem to solve, son, you have to break it down and take it a piece at a time.*

He suddenly realized he wasn't alone after all. He still had Papa with him. He knew exactly what his dad would say in every case.

CHAPTER 2

Right now he was saying, *You get yourself together, boy. You done good figuring out to backtrack, now you put some distance between you and this place.*

Bryan smiled as he got his gear together and whispered, "Yes, Pa."

As he stepped out, the verse he had read returned to him, *I will bring all things to your remembrance.* First his mother and now his father. Comfort indeed.

3

Bryan set a fierce pace most of the day, constantly scanning the countryside as he went, expecting the raiding war party to find him at any moment. He didn't know what he'd do if—

Thundering hoofbeats behind him startled him into spinning around. A mounted brave was right on top of him, leaning down, spear in hand. With no time to think about it, Bryan acted instinctively.

He dodged to the side of the spear, catching the wrist holding it and throwing his weight into it. He didn't know what he'd do next. He was just a boy—no match for a mounted warrior.

The rider, off balance hanging from the horse, couldn't recover from the sudden weight hanging on his arm and went down hard. Bryan knew he had only one chance to get him before the Indian got his breath back. He jumped for him, but the warrior wasn't as stunned as he thought.

Bryan felt the foot in his stomach and felt himself going up and over, landing hard on his back. It was his turn to be stunned. The Indian scrambled to his feet and leaped for him.

The boys in the wagon train had spent many hours wrestling with one another, and Bryan was strong for his age. He had always done well. But he had never had as much riding on the outcome before. He brought his knee up, and the Indian landed solidly on it. It went deep into the Indian's stomach. He let out a great *whoooosh* of air like a locomotive blowing off steam.

He saw the knife and kicked it from the Indian's hand. Bryan scrambled for it, scooping it up as he turned to face his enemy. The Indian was still down on his knees, clutching his stomach. Then it dawned on him; this was no warrior. This was a boy, maybe a year or two younger than himself.

"You speak English?"

The youngster glared at him.

"Guess not."

Bryan lifted his rifle and eased it up to the ready. He made gestures for the boy to lie on his stomach. When he did, Bryan quickly caught up the boy's hands behind him and tied them together with a piece of rawhide string. Then he tied his feet together as well.

He saw the spear lying nearby. *Wait a minute, that's not a spear, it's a stick!*

He looked at the boy with confusion on his face. The boy responded with the same hostile glare.

The horse the boy had been riding had stayed close. The pony's eyes were wild, the whites showing as it breathed heavily after trying to run him down. Bryan cocked the rifle and scanned the horizon expecting more raiders where this one had come from. The minutes passed, but nobody came.

The boy lay there, the fierce look not quite hiding a look of fear, not daring to move with the rifle in Bryan's hand.

"I guess you're out here on your own. That don't sound too smart to me, but then I'm out here on my own too. I *know* that ain't smart, but I got no choice."

The time gave the animal a chance to settle down. Finally Bryan spoke to it. "You're Bobby Jackson's horse, ain't you? You're Patches."

At the sound of his voice the little horse's head jerked up. The animal backed up several steps.

"How about it, boy. Are you Patches?"

The familiar name stopped the horse, but he still eyed Bryan warily. "Reckon there ain't nobody after you."

He took a step toward the horse. The animal matched each step going back, maintaining the interval.

"Now don't be like that, Patches. You know me. I've ridden you before."

The horse didn't seem quite as wild. Bryan continued to talk soothingly, but made no sudden moves.

"Come on Patches. You know me, don't you?"

He took his canteen and poured water in his hat. "I thought maybe you recognized your name, but you sure enough recognize the scent of this water, don't you?"

Patches came slowly forward, put his muzzle into the hat and drank. Bryan rubbed the pony's neck, speaking gently.

"That's a good boy. Reckon you got captured with the rest of the horses?"

A feather was braided into the rope halter. He jerked it out. Some beadwork worked into the halter looked the same as what he had seen on a couple of broken lances at the wagon train. Comanche. He was sure of it.

This one was too young to have participated, but he was a dead cinch to be kin to the ones that did. Anger came over him, a need to take revenge for his parents. It surged to the surface, white-hot, and he felt it in his face and neck.

He looked at the immobilized boy. It would be easy. He let out a deep sigh. But it wouldn't be right. He knew the old phrase that two wrongs don't add up to make a right. He knew what the Book said about "thou shall not kill." He pushed the thought from his mind. It wasn't in him.

He continued to rub and touch the pony, could feel him calm to his touch. There was a handprint on the pony's hip, made in something akin to red paint. That would have to come off too.

"Reckon that's why you're so skittish." He laughed.

Bryan held on to the little horse's bridle and turned back to his captive. "They may come looking for you any time. I better get outta here."

He led Patches over to his gear. Western horses were trained to stand ground hitched if their reins are left hanging down, but he couldn't trust that right now. He tied the rope halter to a good-sized rock as he repacked his gear to go on him, hurrying as best as he could.

He took one blanket from his roll and folded it for a saddle blanket. Then he tied the blanket roll to the strings attached to the saddlebags and threw them on the little horse, which nickered at the familiar weight.

"A saddle would be nice," he muttered. But he had ridden bareback before, many times. It would surely be better than walking.

Bryan smoothed the blanket on the horse's back to protect the horse, not to mention his own rump, and clambered aboard. Patches spun, responding to the pressure of Bryan's knees and the tug on the reins. The pony seemed eager to be away from this place.

Bryan rode back to where the Indian was lying. "I hate to take your horse," he said, "but that's how you got him in the first place, isn't it?"

The hostile look had been replaced by an uncertain look in the boy's eyes. "I know you don't get what I'm saying," Bryan said, "but I can see you're worried I might kill you. It crossed my mind, but I never killed nuthin except to put on the dinner table, and I'm not planning to start now. I can't let you be going after them that hit the wagon train and bringing them back down on me though."

He held the knife up, and the boy's eyes got very wide.

Bryan tossed the knife down not too far from where his captive was lying. "I guess by the time you figure out how to use that to cut yourself loose and walk back to your people, maybe that'll give me time to put enough distance between us to be out of reach."

The boy relaxed. He understood the gesture of the knife and what it meant.

Bryan turned the pony and rode off. He rode back the way the Indian boy had come from. "I know you don't want to go back this way and neither do I, horse, but I need to be sure how you came in. Sure don't wanna run into them that might be chasing you. Gotta make sure I'm going the other way."

The tracks told Bryan the horse had come in on a run from the hills to the southwest. *Good. That means continuing east is still the right thing to do.*

He rode back to where the boy was squirming trying to reach the knife. The fear came back into his eyes as he saw Bryan return. Bryan knew he was afraid he had changed his mind about killing him and laughed as he rode right by him.

He went back to the wagon ruts and set off at a trot. It was a pace the little horse could keep up for a long time. As they went Bryan talked to him to steady him down, or maybe because he found it comforting to have somebody to talk to.

"It took us weeks to get here, fella, but we were only able to make a couple of dozen miles a day with those heavy wagons. I reckon we can cut that time in half traveling light the way we are."

Patches tossed his head, as if agreeing with him.

It was just a pinprick of light when Bryan first saw it. When it had started to get dusk they had slowed to a walk, but hadn't been ready to stop. There was a three-quarter moon, and they could see to travel as long as they took it slow.

The pinprick grew to a dot, then finally became clear that it was a fire back off the wagon track in a little grove of trees.

Bryan tied Patches, cocked his rifle and eased up to see what it was all about. He went so slow and easy that it seemed to take forever to ease up on the camp. There were two forms huddled in blankets around fire burned down to be little more than embers. Bryan couldn't tell anything about them, so he eased closer.

Suddenly he froze as a voice said, "I see you, boy, and I got this here Colt centered smack dab on ya under this blanket. Now you point that old Henry off somewhere else and ease that hammer down on it right careful-like."

Bryan did as the man said, but he eased the little pistol out of his waistband, to conceal it in his palm.

"Now you come on in here and keep both hands where I can see 'em."

The big pistol was outside the blanket now, and there was no doubt it meant business.

"Now sit! I'm gonna need to take yore measure. You just push that rifle away."

The man sat up. He was huge, and Bryan flinched from his sour smell, though he was completely across the clearing from him.

Raven black hair and striking dark eyes peeked out over the hem of the other blanket. A voice said, "Fat Jack, what?"

"You hush, Morning Star. We got us a visitor. I'm having a look at him now. I 'spect he ain't much younger than you are. Ain't that nice? He cocked his head and squinted one eye as he studied Bryan. "What's yore name, boy?"

"Bryan Wheeler, sir."

"Sir? Well ain't that polite. I ain't been sir'd in a long time. What's a sprout like you doing out by yore lonesome?" He glanced out suddenly at the darkness. "You is by yourself, ain'tcha?"

"Yes, sir. I was with a wagon train. A war party hit it while I was out hunting. I guess they surprised them. There's nobody left."

The big man rubbed his chin in thought as he peered off in the distance, though he couldn't see much past the clearing. "You don't say. Injuns, huh? That'd be west of here?"

"Yes, sir. A full day's ride."

"Reckon we'd better swing down more to the south. Don't care to run into no war party." He looked over at Morning Star. "Might be some of your kin, and might not take kindly to me buying you from them trappers."

Bryan heard the hammer let down on the pistol and let out the breath he didn't know he was holding. He tucked the little pistol into his belt behind him, under his vest.

"I guess you be all right." Fat Jack measured him with his eyes, "You ain't totin' no possibles?"

"Got a few things on my horse. I tied him off a ways, out of sight."

"Right sensible of you seeing how things lay out before you come busting in. Reckon you oughta learn how to walk in the woods though before you try it again though." He made a gesture indicating the trees. "I been listening to you coming for quite a spell."

"Really?"

"Yeah, really. Now you go fetch yore stuff, and I'll have Morning Star whip you up something to eat."

"I just got warm," she said in a small voice.

"You do what I tell you afore I fetch you another clout upside the head."

She grimaced, then threw off the blankets and began to pull on a pair of moccasins.

"Sir, there's no reason for that, I'm not—"

He swung toward the boy, a thundercloud look on his face. "Now sonny boy, don't you go to meddling in things that don't concern you, ya hear?"

"Yes, sir."

Morning Star pulled a pot from the saddlebags and busied herself with the task. She made no eye contact with either of them.

She's scared to death of him. Alarms went off in Bryan's head. *What have I walked into here?*

4

"If you're gonna throw in with us," Fat Jack said, "you gonna have to learn that I'm the big he-bull around here, and you hafta to learn to jump when I say frog. You get me, boy?"

"Yes, sir."

"Now go fetch yore things like I told ya."

Bryan walked out where he left Patches. *I got a notion to just climb aboard and put some miles between me and that terrible man.*

Even as he entertained the thought, the fear in those dark eyes nagged at him and he found it wasn't in him to ride off and leave her.

I don't know what I can do, probably nothing, but it looks like she needs help bad. I can't go off and leave her like this.

He untied the little horse and got aboard. "Dunno what I've got us into, boy, but reckon I've got this to do. 'Spect I better hide this money, and I think it best this little pistol remain our secret for a while as well."

He hid a small stash before going back into the camp. He returned to find the girl frying up some fatback and skillet bread. She had a little pot of beans heating as well. There was very little variety to food on the trail.

"I'm sorry to be the cause of so much trouble," he said with an apologetic smile.

She only shook her head.

Fat Jack rolled back into his blankets. A rumbling snore came almost immediately from deep within the rumpled heap.

Bryan whispered, "Is he asleep?"

She nodded. "Long as he snores. If he quits, watch out."

"Did he say your name is Morning Star?"

She found reasons not to look at him. Her skin was like cherry wood and the golden-hued doeskin dress was decorated with delicate beadwork.

"Yes."

"Guess you heard mine?"

"Yes, you said Bryan?" She made it a question as she made very brief eye contact, quickly looking back to the beans she stirred on the edge of the fire.

"Bryan Wheeler." He glanced at the mound of blankets again. "Did he say he bought you from some trappers?"

"He bought me. I was with my brother and my uncle going back to the land of the endless grass. The trappers came upon us unawares and shot my family, then took me with them."

"That's awful."

She shrugged, "It is how life is." She lowered her voice even more. "I must mind or he beats me."

Fat Jack got quiet. She looked at the big man, waiting for the reassuring rumble which soon came, then put a plate in front of Bryan. The dark eyes reflected the light from the fire as they bored into his. "You shouldn't have come back. You should have ridden on."

"I thought on it."

He took a bite of the beans. He hadn't realized he was so hungry. "This is good. Thanks."

She gave a semblance of a smile in response. She pulled out a small sack and reached in to get some of the contents between her thumb and forefinger. She sprinkled it over the beans, repeating it a second time. "Dried peppers," she explained. "Very good on beans. He does not want me to use them, but I do."

He avoided eye contact as he said, "I would have ridden on if it hadn't been for you. I thought you needed some help."

The semblance of a smile blossomed into the genuine article. "It is true, I need help, but it will take more than a boy to give it to me."

"You're right, I probably can't do nuthin, but I don't know. I just couldn't ride off . . . I just couldn't."

"You have a good heart. But it has led you into danger."

"I just felt I had it to do. It's how I was raised."

She touched his hand. "I fear you will live to regret it."

When Bryan finished, he quickly cleaned up his dishes, built up the fire again and arranged his blankets across the fire from the big man. He laid down with his clothes on, going to sleep as soon as his head hit the ground.

Bryan awoke to find Fat Jack going through his things. Bryan had the little pistol in his hand under the blanket. He raised his head to look at Fat Jack and said, "Find what you're looking for?"

Fat Jack made no apology. "What you got all these here letters for? They ain't to you. And there ain't no money in them."

Bryan raise up on his elbow. "I'm gonna write their kin to tell them what happened."

Fat Jack wiped his nose on his sleeve, letters clutched in a grimy hand. "Reckon it'll fetch you a reward?"

"No."

"Then whatcha want to go to all that trouble for?"

"I owe it to them. They were good to me."

He cocked his head, disbelief on his face, "They're dead, boy, don'tcha get that?" He stomped off.

Morning Star said, "It is not in him to understand doing something for someone without getting anything out of it."

Bryan watched as she again fried up fatback and skillet bread. She performed the tasks effortlessly, done so often that they didn't even require thought. That freed her mind to think of other things. She cast a sideways glance at Bryan and caught him watching her. She quickly looked away.

Bryan watched her brush the hair out of her eyes with the back of her hand. She seemed so distant, as if she were one hundred miles away.

I wish we were one hundred miles away, he thought. *If I could just find a way to get her away from him. It couldn't be a way that would put her at risk though.*

Bryan knew Fat Jack wouldn't search him again, so he picked up the money he had stashed and put it in his saddlebags. As he did he noticed the envelopes holding the letters to the folks back home were empty. He held one up and said, "Where are the letters that were in these?"

"Wood was wet, I need some paper to get the fire going."

Bryan jerked upright. "Paper . . . you wouldn't . . ." He looked at the bundle of letters.

"Don't get yoreself in no uproar. I saved you the envelopes. They're what have the addresses on them."

Bryan lost control. He launched himself at the big man. Fat Jack grinned as Bryan came at him and backhanded him into a tree as easy as swatting a fly. Bryan reached behind him to close his hand on the little 32. They stared at each other, then slowly Bryan released his grip on the pistol.

No, he's ready now and I'm no match for him.

Fat Jack's grin widened as he saw Bryan's shoulders sag. "That's better, boy. We'll break you to halter yet." He turned to walk toward where Morning Star watched stoically.

"My name's Bryan, not boy."

Fat Jack stopped in midstride, turned with exaggerated slowness to focus hard eyes on Bryan. "You want some more of this while I'm in the mood to dish it out, *boy*?"

"No, sir."

Bryan wiped blood from the corner of his mouth and looked at it before he wiped it on the grass.

"That's better."

The big man resumed waddling over to where Morning Star finished up the food. He snatched up both pans and walked over to sit on a log. He dug at them with his fingers, seemingly getting as much on his face and in his coarse beard as in his mouth. The noise he made sounded like some wild animal. He finished and tossed the pans down.

"I left a little of that grub for you," he said as if he had done them a favor. "You two split it between you."

He picked up Bryan's rifle. "And I better hang onto this old Henry for a while."

Bryan knew he was a prisoner now, every bit as much as the girl. When Fat Jack took his rifle from him, he took away his ability to ride off at the same time. Not that he would leave the girl, but he hated to not have the choice.

5

Bryan started the next day with a solid boot in his ribs that took his breath. He looked up to see the face he had already learned to hate.

"Roll outta there, boy. The sun's already coming up. You should have already had that fire stoked by now. From now on you have that done before I get out of them blankets. I hate to have to get up to a cold camp."

Bryan backed away from him, scowling. "I don't answer to you. What do you think I am, a slave?"

Fat Jack found the attempt at defiance amusing, his grin yellow and snaggle-toothed. His breath was putrid. "I thought we got that settled last night, boy. We need to go over it again?"

Not smart, Bryan. You got to bide your time.

He rubbed his sore ribs. "No sir, I understand. I just don't like to be kicked awake. Makes me testy."

The humor went out of Fat Jack's grin. "You buck too quick, boy. We gonna have to break you of that."

"Yes, sir."

CHAPTER 5

Bryan moved over and started to build the fire. Morning Star immediately busied herself preparing breakfast, but he could feel her eyes dart to him constantly.

"You should not make him mad," she whispered. "There is much meanness in him."

"Oh, I think I have some idea," Bryan rubbed his sore ribs again.

Morning Star put on coffee and started skillet cakes. Fat Jack walked over to put the pack back on the mule. "Come here, boy. You know how to put a diamond hitch on a mule?"

"No."

"Time you learned. Packing this mule in the morning is gonna be your job from now on." He gave the animal a pat on the back, raising a cloud of dust, "and if you don't do it right this critter will just shuck this stuff off. That means you'll have to do it all over again."

Bryan moved to the other side of the mule, keeping the beast between them. "I do this after I get the fire started, I suppose?"

"Nacherly. You're catching on."

"And the fact that I wasn't planning on traveling any farther with you . . ."

"Don't enter into it. My conscience would never let me be if I let a button like you go off on your own unprotected. Reckon it's up to me to take care of you."

"If you're taking care of me, why is it I'm taking over all these chores?"

"Good training, boy. What with your folks gone, somebody has to finish your raising."

"And that would be you?"

"Exactly. Can I help it if I've got such a big heart?"

By the time they trailed out, the sky was beginning to turn gray with a few crimson streaks showing in the scattered clouds. Fat Jack led the way, and Bryan brought up the rear, leading the pack mule. Fat Jack said he knew Bryan couldn't run without his rifle, so he wasn't worried about him.

The rising sun lit up the endless grass that rose knee high on the horses. The vista went on as far as he could see; the gently rolling hills made it look like waves on a pale yellow ocean. It looked like a field of ripe grain planted by a patient farmer who plowed so close that his furrows didn't even show.

I reckon it was, Bryan thought. *I 'spect the Lord planted this Himself.*

He looked at the girl riding ahead of him. *Why am I doing this? For her? She's nothing to me. I should have lit out as soon as I saw how mean that character is.*

But he knew there was something in him that wouldn't let that happen. He didn't understand it, but he was committed all the same.

They rode all day, stopping only at rare intervals to rest the horses and eat a little jerky and hard tack. At these stops, they sat in silence, ignoring each other, caught up in their own thoughts. It was nearly dusk when they came upon a small stream, and it was there Fat Jack decided to night camp.

6

"You got any kin, boy?" Fat Jack used his sheath knife to cut chunks from an apple as he stared at Bryan across the campfire. He trapped the chunks against the knife blade with his thumb to slip them into his mouth. The apple showed tinges of brown, so it wasn't very fresh.

Bryan didn't mind that the fat man hadn't offered him any of it. He tried not to look at the flecks of apple in Fat Jack's beard.

Not that I know of, Bryan thought. *Probably not the right answer though. I think it's best to keep him off guard a bit, maybe have him think there's somebody who might miss me.* "Yes, sir, back east. I'm headed the wrong way to get back to them."

"Oh, it ain't like that, son. We're gonna get you back to your loved ones when we get somewhere where we can ship you off safely." The big man sat there for a moment, then added, "Wonder if there's a reward for your safe return?"

Oh yeah, I believe that, all right. "I'm not your son," he said aloud. "And I don't know about a reward."

But he did know. All the relations he had were lying out on the prairie back behind him, and he hadn't even been able to give them a decent burial. The tears threatened to come again as he thought about it.

Fat Jack popped the last bite of apple into his mouth and pointing with the blade said, "Don't rile me, boy. You know I can make it unpleasant for you if you rile me."

The big man turned his attention to the task of finishing off the beans in the pot. Bean juice ran down his chin, mixing with the apple. He wiped it off with a meaty hand, then cleaned the hand front and back on his pant leg.

Bryan looked sullen. *Disgusting.* "What do I have to do to get you to call me by my name? My name is Bryan."

The big man just smiled his ugly grin, tossed the now-empty pot over at Morning Star and rolled up in his blankets. She picked up the pot as she cleaned up from the meal.

Bryan moved over by her and said, "Looks like he didn't bother to leave anything this time."

She whispered, "I am used to that. Once he is asleep, I have something put aside for us."

He picked up the now empty pot to help her clean up.

"Don't bother," she said, "wasn't much, and I'm about through."

He ignored her and dried the plates as she pulled them out of the little wash pan.

"Now ain't that sweet?"

They looked over to see Fat Jack looking over his shoulder at them. "You gonna make somebody a good wife, boy."

He turned his back to them again.

They finished and Bryan sat down on a log they had pulled up to the fire. Deep rumbling began to come from the blankets. She got up and retrieved some food, heating it over the fire. It looked better than what she had given Fat Jack.

She split the food into two plates and came over to sit down next to him. It was the first time she had been that close to him, and he found it a little disconcerting.

They didn't look at each other, but occupied themselves eating, doing it quickly, as if Fat Jack might awake any moment and take it from them. They stared into the fire as they ate.

"Why do you stay with him?" Bryan asked.

"Why do you?"

"I told you."

She looked down. "I'm afraid to leave. He'd come after me. He would hurt me much."

They sat in silence for a long time, continuing to stare into the fire.

There has to be some way to get her away from him. He thought as he fingered the little gun in his belt.

No, I don't think I have it in me to kill him.

She seemed to sense what he was thinking, "We could knock him out and leave him tied and afoot."

Bryan shook his head, "No, that'd make him so mad that he'd never give up chasing us. Besides, what would I do with you?"

She smiled. "You need not worry about me. If we can get away and leave him afoot, I can get to my people. You take the pack animal, and he will follow you."

"What do I do when he catches up to me?"

"When I reach my people, he will follow you no more."

"Now look. He's a snake, but I don't want to see him hurt."

"It is not for you to worry. Help me get away. My people will take it from there."

He knew what that meant, and it didn't sit well with him. He sat and thought on it. Maybe it was between them. Maybe that was the right of it.

She got up to clean the dishes, but waved him away as he started to rise to help.

He got out his Bible. He found comfort in his reading tonight, but he found no answers.

She gave him a curious look as he opened the little book and turned to his marker. She spread her blankets and settled in.

While Bryan packed the mule, Morning Star finished cleaning up. Fat Jack lingered over breakfast making disgusting noises. One of the last things to pack was the big cast iron skillet.

Fat Jack paid him no attention, concentrating on eating all that had been cooked for all three of them. Morning Star finished cleaning the skillet and handed it to Bryan. He turned to take it to the pack horse. As he passed Fat Jack, Bryan turned and swung the heavy pan as hard as he could.

It clanged like the Liberty Bell, and Fat Jack's eyes rolled up into his head as he toppled off the log. Bryan moved quickly to tie his arms and legs and take his pistol and hunting knife.

"I hope I didn't kill him," he looked down at the big man. "I hit him awful hard."

She got close to the big man's face, "He breathes."

Her hand slipped down to pull the big Bowie knife from its sheath and raised it to plunge into his chest. Bryan caught her wrist and took the knife from her. "I know you got every right to want to do that," he said, "but I just can't let you do it."

She nodded. "It is for you to say. For now."

He tossed Fat Jack's hand gun across the clearing. "I can't leave him unprotected."

She walked over and picked it up. "When my people come for him, I do not want them hurt."

Bryan thought about his Bible reading the night before, something about a man reaping what he sows. It was out of his hands now.

Bryan watched her ride away. She had turned her nose up at the saddle and rode bareback with only a blanket. She rode tall and proud, nothing like the girl he had seen in camp the past few days. He smiled. Simply knowing she was free of Fat Jack had given her back her pride. He turned his thoughts to his own situation.

When I first found myself alone, I imagined my father telling me what to do. I was sure he would tell me to go back the way I came . . . to go the way I knew. It ain't the same this time. Last time I had a set wagon trail, and I knew it like the back of my hand. Only now, there ain't no trail as such and the way we've been traveling, our back trail is something of a blur. Guess I don't feel confident about it at all.

He sighed deeply, *but I know if I keep on going the way I'm going that I'll hit Oklahoma Territory, or Texas. I've got plenty of provisions, for sure without his big gut to fill, so I figure I'm good until I run into some town or something.*

7

Nothing is as easy as it sounds.

Bryan rode steadily, keeping the sun off his left shoulder in the morning, off his right in the afternoon. It should have worked.

He came across tracks—three shod horses. They made him nervous.

He continued to ride through the tall grass, belly high to the horses. He found a camp. It was a white man's camp with a fire built next to a log. Wait a minute! This was his own camp. He was riding in circles. The tracks of the three horses were his own.

He was lost.

As long as he was here he might as well noon here. He was dejected as he sat on the piece of deadfall and made himself a small fire. Not only was he sure he was lost, but Bryan also couldn't shake the feeling that he was being watched. He had been feeling it as he rode, but even more so since he had stopped.

He heard a small rustling in the tall grass and his breath began to come fast. *I'm just a boy, I'm not ready for this.*

Suddenly there was a scurrying sound, and he struggled to get to his feet. *Oh, why did I get down so far that I can't move fast.*

Someone rushed up behind him. He glanced over his shoulder as he struggled to rise. *It's an Indian!*

Bryan spun and took the Indian down as he got close.

It was an Indian, all right, a very small Indian. Bryan now sat on the intruder's stomach, pinning his arms, but the youngster struggled with all his might.

"Settle down," Bryan commanded between bouts of laughter. "I ain't gonna hurt ya. You speak our lingo?"

The youngster ceased his efforts. "I speak it. The soldiers at the fort teach it to me."

"Well, I ain't gonna let you up until I find out what's going on. You been shadowing me?"

"You knew?" A scowl crossed the small face.

"I never saw you, but I felt you."

The scowl turned to consternation. "Then I am shamed," his chin dropped onto his chest. "You were not supposed to know."

"Were you planning on killing me?"

"I did not wish that. I tried to count coup on you and disappear as fast as I had come."

Bryan didn't get it. "Count coup?"

"It is where we get close enough to touch an enemy yet get away."

"Am I your enemy?" Bryan appeared a little hurt by the possibility.

"You are stranger. It is close enough."

Bryan got up, dusting himself off with his hat. "So that's what that Comanche boy did back down the road. I couldn't figure it out, but I thought he was trying to kill me." He smiled at the boy. "I guess you mean me no harm. Aren't there any full grown Indians out this way?"

"I do not understand."

"It's just that I keep running into pint-sized versions. I guess I'm not that eager to find big ones though. Are there others with you?"

Bryan looked around as he retrieved his rifle.

The little guy rose slowly, making no effort to remove the dust that coated him. "I am alone."

"Aren't you too young to be off on your own like this."

He pulled back indignantly, "My village is a half day ride. I am out learning the skills I must have to be a man," his chin came up, "to become a warrior." He made a sign of his index finger in front of his face, palm in and changed it into loose fists palms toward each other.

Bryan smiled at him, replacing his hat. "You sure talk good American to be an Injun. What was that you did with your hands?"

"It is sign language, it allows tribes to understand each other even if the language is different. But I am Cherokee. Our people are good friends to the *yoneg*," his gesture included them both, "the white man."

"Then why do you need to learn to be a warrior?"

The boy shrugged, "It is how it has always been. Other tribes are not so peaceful. If we were not strong, they would attack us. But we are strong." He made a motion as if he were breaking a small stick. "The Cherokee are feared as warriors."

"I see. Why did it shame you for me to know you were there?"

"In tsalgi, in the Cherokee tongue, we say *atsalagi tsigi eligwu g'waltadodi ayonega dukan'i*. Roughly translated it means 'a Cherokee can disappear from white men's eyes.' It is a skill I must master to become a warrior."

He lowered his head and spoke softly. "I am not yet ready."

Bryan squatted on his heels to get down on his level. "Weren't you afraid?"

His head dropped even lower as he admitted, "I was." He held out his hand palm out, then curved the fingers down.

"Fearing weapons is nothing to be ashamed of."

The chin came up again, "Fearing anything is something to be ashamed of."

"Mighty brave talk for a tadpole. How old are you?"

The chin went even higher, "I have seen eleven summers."

"And you're off on your own far from your village? I'm here with a half dozen guns and still scared to death."

"Why do you fear?" he asked Bryan as if he couldn't quite believe it would be true.

"The unknown, I guess. I don't really know where I am."

"You are in the Indian territory. The lands of the five civilized tribes lie to the east. To the west are plains Indians, Comanche and Kiowa. They are fearsome warriors. They are not friends to the white man. Or to the Cherokee. If they find me, I die." He swept his hands to the directions as he indicated them.

"I owe you an apology. You are truly brave."

The youngster fought off showing a smile. "It is good I found you instead of them. I am not ready to meet them."

"What's your name?"

"I am called Red Eagle."

"I'm Bryan. Are you hungry?"

Red Eagle nodded once, holding his hand palm up at his stomach then moving it as if he was cutting himself in two, "I have not yet taken time to find food."

Bryan was fascinated by the movement of his hands, and the gestures made sense. "I'm about to eat; come share it with me."

"I think I would like that."

The young Cherokee had worked up a ravenous appetite and showed it in the ferocity with which he ate, as well as in the quantity he consumed.

"I'm glad you feel comfortable enough to eat your fill. A lot of people would pick at it and not eat as much as they wanted trying to be polite."

He paused, fingers full of food half way to his mouth. "Not eat? When there is food? I do not understand. With the Cherokee, food is not owned by anyone, but provided for all our use. Our food is taken to the storehouse and those who need it take what they require. Those who raise crops or kill meat take them there. No Cherokee, or anyone who might be with us, would go hungry unless all are hungry."

"I see. That's not a bad way. Folks oughta take care of one another," Bryan said. "Are there any towns around here?"

"The closest would be Turkey Creek. It is to the southeast." Red Eagle pointed with a piece of hard tack, his cheek full of food. "Our village is due east. There are some farms and ranches between here and the town."

"Thanks. It feels good to have some idea of where we are. How do you keep your directions straight so well? I'm not having much luck at it."

"Early in the morning and late in the afternoon," he swept his hand to show the positions of the sun, "directions are very clear, marked by the rising and setting of the sun. It is at these times that we should select a marker in the distance to guide our travel, to keep us traveling straight. In the middle of the day, the sun gives us little clue. It is easy at this time to lose our direction."

"So that's it. I think I've lost my way several times. Once I even came back on my own tracks where I'd traveled in a circle."

"It is easy to do." Red Eagle popped the last bite into his mouth, licked the tips of his fingers, then wiped them on his breeches.

"And you don't carry any weapon except that small bow and arrows?"

He shook his head, then turned slightly to make the small blade visible on his hip. "I have my knife, but other than that, no."

Man, I made a mistake there. This little rabbit had teeth and I didn't even know it. He coulda stuck me with that thing. "And you feed yourself with it?"

"Hunger can make the eye keen and the hand steady."

"Even at your age there is much you could teach me."

"It is mostly found in the way we look at things." He made a sign pointing to his eyes then sweeping his hand away. "For the white man nature is an adversary, something to be endured or conquered. To the Indian it is all part of us, it gives us what we need."

"You say nature, don't you mean God?"

"I was thinking of the land, but yes, that was given to us by the Great Provider."

"Great Provider? Is that the same as God?"

"I think so. Our people have believed in the Great Provider long before the white man came with the Bible. I have read in this Bible some. I think perhaps they are one and the same."

"So you aren't a Christian?"

He seemed to relax for the first time. Even while eating he had appeared poised for flight. He sat down cross-legged. "Many Cherokee are Christian. It is part of why I practice, so I may become a man. My father will not yet allow me to embrace this religion."

Bryan looked at him intently. "Your father is not a Christian?"

Red Eagle nodded, "Yes, he is. But it is our way for me to first prove I am a man. So he may be sure that I am not just accepting without understanding."

"How old do you have to be?"

"It is not a matter of age. It is a matter of skill and understanding. A matter of proving myself."

"For us we don't have to be any particular age, long as we're old enough to understand Jesus died to save us."

"I know of this," he nodded, "I'm eager to learn more."

They retrieved Red Eagle's pinto and set out again, riding abreast of one another. Bryan was still very curious. "How come your father isn't out here with you overseeing this training?"

Red Eagle held himself very erect on the little horse. "It is not his place to do so."

"I don't understand."

"It is my uncle, my mother's brother, who must do this. My father has those he is responsible for training, but not me."

Bryan shook his head. "I don't get it, why would it be that way?"

"I have thought on this. Perhaps it is thought he would be too hard on his own son, or perhaps not hard enough. Whatever the reason, it has always been so."

Bryan scowled, "But sending you out on your own . . ."

"My uncle, Laughing Bear, has spent much time with me. He has shown me the tracks of those I must respect, the tracks of those on which I may feed." He closed his hand and moved the tips of his fingers past his mouth several times. "He has shown me the things I may eat and those that will harm me.

This training began at an early age. He did not just cast me adrift to see if I might swim."

"That's sort of how I feel, cast adrift," Bryan said. "My father showed me a lot, but I didn't know how much I needed to learn and how quick. Just one day he wasn't there any more, and, yes, it did feel like it was sink or swim."

"It is a hard way to have to learn." He struck his left palm with his right fist.

Bryan's eyes followed each gesture with intense interest. "But you know, I can still hear my dad when I need to."

Red Eagle smiled, something he didn't allow himself to do often. "I understand. I can hear my uncle and my father in the wind when I stop to listen." He cupped his hand to his ear, "Their voices come to me when my heart is ready."

"That's it exactly."

"Perhaps it is time. When my uncle thinks I am ready, he sends me out to test my skills. Would it have made a difference if your father had told you this before you went out for the last time? If he had said you were ready to face life and sent you to go try your skills?"

"Yes," Bryan said, "it would have made a big difference. I would have had questions before I left, but I know he would have reassured me."

Red Eagle looked at him intently, "Would he have told you that you were ready?"

"I don't know."

Red Eagle shook his head, "I think you do."

"You don't act like an eleven-year-old. I keep getting the feeling you're older than I am, not younger. But to answer your question, my dad wouldn't have felt I was old enough to leave home. Still, had someone had been able to forecast what was about to happen, I suppose he would have said I could handle it."

"Then you have your answer. You are the same as I. We test our wings. I think we will fly." He extended his hands flat and imitated a bird's wings.

"I'm sure of it," Bryan said.

They heard it long before they saw anything. "What is that noise?" Bryan stood high in his stirrups, but the added height didn't help, he still couldn't see. "Sounds like somebody banging on a washtub. Actually, it sounds like a whole bunch of people banging on tubs."

Red Eagle said, "I know this noise. It is the professor."

Bryan continued to stare into the distance, "Who is the professor?"

"You will see." He pointed to his eyes, then in the direction the noise came from.

They rode over the rise to find a peculiar wagon rolling along. Pots and pans, harness rigging, and all types of merchandise hung on the sides heralding the eminent arrival of the traveling peddler. The old man driving the rig had on a tall stovepipe hat and a khaki-colored duster. He had a stub of a pipe in his mouth and wore a two-day growth of gray-white beard.

He spotted them coming and pulled up. "Red Eagle, what brings you out this way? Who is it you have with you? I sure didn't expect to run onto anybody out in these parts."

"I was out doing my drills. I counted coup as I was taught," the boy shrugged, "but not very well I fear."

The old man tied off the reins on the wagon brake, tapped out the contents of his pipe over the side and began to repack it from a small pouch.

"Takes time to get good at it," he said. "You're in too much of a hurry. I'm on my way over to do a little trading with your family."

He pulled his hat off to flick some dust from it. "Guess I should introduce myself." He gave a mischievous sideways glance at them. "I am Professor Harold Donovan, purveyor of merchandise extraordinaire and the inventor of Donovan's Miracle Tonics. Guess you youngsters don't have much in the way of aches and pains as of yet, but if you did, I have something to cure whatever might ail you."

He put his hat back on and stepped down to the hub of the front wheel, then to the ground carrying a pail with him. He stepped back to fill it with water from the barrel.

Bryan said, "Snake oil salesman?"

"Humph. Don't be impertinent, son. Years of research have gone into the development of this fine product."

He moved to hold the pail where the mules could drink, first one and then the other. "And who would you be?"

"I'm Bryan Wheeler."

The professor came around the team, patting one of the big animals on the neck. He showed no surprise, but said casually, "Carol Sue, we got visitors."

Blonde hair and the most remarkable blue eyes looked around the wagon cover. "Yes? Oh, hello Red Eagle."

Bryan stammered, "Uh, hello."

She looked at him, awaiting an introduction.

"I'm . . . I'm Bryan."

"Hello."

"If you're going to live out this way, you're going to have to affect a bit more drawl into your voice," the professor said. "T'will make you easier to understand. Where's the rest of your party?"

Bryan said huskily, "May I have a drink of that water?" He stepped down, twisting one way, then the other to relieve the stiffness from hours in the saddle.

"Of course." Carol Sue reached into the back, pulled out a cup, and handed it to the professor who filled it and offered it to him.

Bryan answered as he accepted the cup. "I'm it. Wagon train was wiped out. I'm the only one that got away."

The professor shook his head. "How tragic. This land can be almighty hard. Where did this happen?"

He handed back the cup, "We were bound for Oregon."

"You don't say! You, lad, have come a far piece already and seem a bit young to be undertaking such a journey on your own, if you don't mind me saying."

The professor asked if he wanted his cup refilled with a gesture. Bryan shook his head to say no, as did Red Eagle.

"I wouldn't argue that, but it wasn't of my choosing," Bryan said. "I've been on my own for some time now. Wouldn't object to some company for a change though."

"Nor would I, son, nor would I."

"My name's Bryan," he made a point of repeating his name again. He took a couple of quick steps to offer his hand as he explained. "I recently had a bad experience with a man who constantly called me boy or son."

"Then I shan't do that, Bryan. If you have come this far still in possession of your hair, you have certainly earned the right to be addressed by your proper name."

Bryan retrieved his hand. "I appreciate that."

"I was just contemplating yon grove of trees for a night camp. I fear we have little to offer in the way of victuals, as I have not had the chance to stock provisions lately, but you are welcome to what we have."

"Victuals? Does that mean food?"

"It does."

"Actually I'm pretty well fixed for food, though I'm not the best of cooks."

"My culinary skill is minimal at best, but fortunately Carol Sue is quite the chef."

"You sure talk funny," Bryan said.

The professor removed his hat and held it as a salute. "Ah, the product of a Harvard education. I was trained in elocution and the business skills to run a major institution, but I was also cursed with a pair of feet that have a severe tendency to wander. I find I must always know what is just over the horizon."

"A gypsy, huh?" Bryan said.

The professor pulled out a red bandana, wiped his face, then his hatband before he replaced the hat and gave it a tap to seat it firmly. He went on to mop his face and neck before folding and replacing bandana in his coat pocket. "Not by birth or genealogy, but it must be said that I am a wandering man and would certainly be a kindred spirit to a member of a gypsy tribe."

Bryan shook his head. "At times it sounds like you're talking a foreign language."

"I shall try to restrain my vocabulary, my young friend. Or perhaps we shall enhance yours a bit instead . . . or both."

"What's a vocab . . . what you said?"

The professor held up a finger as if pointing skyward, "It is a word that means one's store of words. The words you can call upon to express yourself."

"You sure got a lot of them."

"Yes, my friend, that I do."

The professor turned and said, "Red Eagle, it's starting to come on twilight, you best return to your family lest they worry about you. Tell your people we'll be there sometime tomorrow."

He replaced the pail.

"Now my young friends, shall we see what hospitality yon clearing offers?"

9

"Carol Sue, you have outdone yourself." The professor wiped the corners of his mouth with his bandana.

Carol Sue's cheeks colored slightly as she gave a small curtsy, "Thank you."

Professor Donovan changed the subject. "All of the gear that came off that horse seems to be from the same person. A man of mammoth proportions, I would say."

"If that means big, Fat Jack was all of that and more," Bryan said.

"Fat Jack? A relative?"

Bryan shook his head, "A terrible man. When I came on him, he had a young Indian girl he had bought like she was a horse or something. I helped her get away, and I'm afraid I stole his gear. I didn't really want to steal it, but I couldn't afford to leave him able to come after me or that girl."

The professor looked thoughtful. "Afoot in Indian country, and the maiden riding for her family? My young friend, it would have been kinder if you had put a bullet between his eyes."

"The idea occurred to me, but I couldn't do it. The best I could do was get me and her away from him. What happens after that is out of my hands. I hope he makes it."

"Admirable. Admirable, indeed. Well, it would seem you have no need of his belongings."

"I got no use for them, that's for sure."

"Buying and selling is my business, young Bryan. Let us see if we may reach an accommodation."

"Does that mean we're gonna dicker?"

The professor nodded, "It does."

Bryan turned back around, "Professor, let's us dicker."

They went through Fat Jack's things and determined what he wished to keep and what he had no use for. Bryan wanted to keep the pistol, and the big man's Winchester was a far better rifle than his old Henry.

The professor sniffed. "Whew! These clothes will take a tremendous amount of sanitizing, but they are in good shape. I do experience a lot of demand for larger size clothing. While I go through this merchandise, perhaps you would care to browse. I'm amenable to paying a fair price, of course, but I far prefer to barter if you find things which might perhaps be of use."

Money changed hands, but the trade included a lot of essentials. Bryan traded off the mule, but kept the horse. "I'm going to turn it over to the law when we get to a town," he said. "Last thing I need is to be accused of being a horse thief."

After the trade they were sitting around the fire when Bryan asked, "Is Carol Sue your daughter?"

"She is my ward. Actually we are all each other has in the world. Her parents just died, so after the funeral I took her under my wing as it were. This is her first trip out in the west. We are getting to know one another, aren't we my dear?"

The professor walked over to where Bryan was putting the finishing touches on his travel gear. Streaks of light were just beginning to show in the east, the fire was made, and Carol Sue called them to breakfast.

"Whatever his faults, and they appear to be legion," the professor noted, "this Fat Jack character certainly taught you to be an efficient traveling companion. Up before the first rays of dawn, packed and ready, know exactly what to do and when. I presume this is the result of his tutelage?"

"Mostly I got it from my dad. But Fat Jack taught me to pack a horse."

"I'm sure he did. Shall we attend yon fair lady?"

The camp chairs were arranged around a board on a barrel. Hot cups of coffee gave off steam around plates already served. Bryan couldn't believe his eyes.

"Eggs? Are those eggs?"

She laughed. "I found several nests over in those reeds. Ducks. It's all right. They're fresh."

"What a treat," the professor said. He stepped to the wagon. "And may I contribute some orange marmalade to this feast?"

"A bit fancy for skillet bread," she said.

"Not at all, my dear, not at all."

They sat down and he said, "Bryan, would you like to say grace for us?"

"I'd like that. I was brought up that way, but Fat Jack wouldn't allow it. He called it foolishness. I've missed it."

They bowed their heads while he did the honors. "Heavenly Father, thank You for this day and the many blessings You have given us. We pray You will go with us and watch over us as we travel. Bless this food and the hands that prepared it. Forgive us our sins, for we ask it in Jesus' name, amen."

They woofed down breakfast, cleaned up, then the professor helped Carol Sue to the high seat of the wagon.

Bryan mounted and fell in beside the wagon as it pulled out. The mule and the packhorse were tied to the tailgate of the wagon. It was much easier traveling that way.

The professor held the reins loosely, leaning back in the seat where he had a clear view of both youngsters. "I believe the time has come, my young friends, to discuss our destination. After we visit the village, there are some ranches that I intend to call upon to merchandise my wares. You see, I know the countryside from pillar to post and make my way down selected routes when the spirit moves me to do so. I am generally well received as I give a fair product at an honest price."

"Reckon it's good to have such a reputation." Bryan rode with his hands crossed on his saddle horn.

"Ah, Bryan, there is little in life as important as a good name. Now let us talk of your itinerary. Do you have time to travel such a circuitous route, or is there somewhere you need to be by a particular time?"

"Nobody looking for me at any particular time. In fact," he made a dour face, "I got nobody to look for me at all."

"Excellent, a fellow free spirit. . . . I love it! There's nothing like having the whole world at your disposal," he swept his hand to take in the entire horizon, "and having the wherewithal and the inclination to make the most of it."

Bryan shook his head, "You know, you use so many big words I've never heard of, but hanged if I'm not starting to sort out the meaning of some of them even if I don't know what they are."

"It's called getting the meaning out of the context. Even if you aren't familiar with the word, the way I use it suggests the meaning. Still, as we are working on your vocabulary, if you want a word defined, don't hesitate to ask."

"Vocabulary." Bryan held up his index finger. "I got that one, that's the word that means all the words we know?"

"Precisely, very good, and in learning that you added the word to your own vocabulary."

"Shoot, I didn't even know I had one to add it to."

"Is that the village?" Carol Sue asked.

"Yes it is, my dear. Not what you expected is it?" the professor said.

"Well, no, I thought there would be teepees and naked savages. That just looks like a small town."

"The Cherokee are farmers," the professor said, "they build towns around a meetinghouse, much like we do a courthouse. They share the farms and work them together. They wear turbans that somewhat remind me of an Arab."

Bryan looked puzzled, "What's an Arab?"

"Someone from a country far, far away—the middle East, actually."

She shook her head in wonder. "You know so much."

"Education is a wonderful thing. I suppose both of you have had your own education somewhat curtailed."

"Curtailed?" Bryan didn't get that one. "Does that mean we haven't had much?"

"Exactly, cut short."

"I didn't get to go to a regular school," Carol Sue said, "but Mama worked really hard at it. I can do my letters and cipher. I read pretty well."

"I went to a one-room schoolhouse," Bryan said, "except during planting and harvest, of course. On the wagon train we had a schoolteacher with us. She made us do our lessons every night."

"Marvelous, marvelous. Perhaps we shall have occasion to further it a bit if we continue in each other's company."

"But I've made it through the forms," Bryan continued. "Reckon I've about got my schooling done."

"Me too. Mama said I had pretty much learned what I needed to become a good wife."

"Oh, my young friends, that's not the right attitude to have. I've gone through school; I've attended the university; I've read books galore. I trade for them constantly and will read anything. At first when I got to college I thought I had about learned all a man could know. By the time I got out I understood that there is more to learn than a man could assimilate in a lifetime if he studied all of every day of his life."

"Why would somebody want to know that much?" Bryan asked.

"Knowledge is power. The more you know, the more you can do. And not all of it comes from books. I heard you milking our Cherokee friend for information. He had much you wanted to learn, did he not?"

"Yes."

"Studying human nature, learning to farm or ranch or be a good mother, all are part of the learning experience, and all education is not to be found in books. If you would be all you can be, my friends, never cease to be a student. Even the village idiot has something to teach us if we are open to learn. Ask yourself of everyone you meet, what does this person have to teach me? Read every book you can to see what it contains that you might want to know. You will see. Knowledge is wonderful, the more you acquire, the more you want. And the more prepared you are for whatever life might bring to you."

"You've made me think, Professor," Bryan admitted.

"Wonderful, if you will just continue to do so . . . ah, we come to the village. The house I am looking for is just ahead on the right. It belongs to Lily Walking Dove, a white woman who has lived among the Cherokee most of her life. She is now a *Ghigau*, which means beloved woman, and means she is a healer held in high regard by her people. I flatter myself that my little remedies have much to do with her reputation, and much that she knows has made its way back into my remedies."

As they neared, the woman who came out to greet them was of uncommon beauty, dark haired and dark eyed, burned brown by the sun until her complexion neared that of the natives in her village. She wore an ankle-length skirt with a loose tunic hanging down over it secured by a silver concho belt. Her hair was nearly to her waist, but was gathered into a single pony tail which hung down the front of her tunic. Soft white, high top moccasins were on her feet. She moved with a grace that was such that she appeared to float out through the door.

"Professor," she said with a smile in her voice, "Welcome *kanalee*, old friend," she made a sign of shaking her own hand. "It has been too long."

"That it has, Lily. Let me present my two new traveling companions, Carol Sue Finney and Bryan Wheeler. This is the pride of the Cherokee Nation, Lily Walking Dove."

She graciously inclined her head. "I am pleased."

She swept an arm back toward her house. "Will you allow me to share my simple hospitality?"

"Bryan and I must tend to the stock; however, we'll leave Carol Sue to your tender ministrations."

"Very well, Professor, we'll look to preparing a meal."

The two began cutting vegetables and Carol Sue set about plucking a chicken. Finally she looked over at Lily and said, "I know this must be bad manners to ask, but—"

"But you're very curious as to what a white woman is doing living among the Cherokee?"

Carol Sue ducked her head and the intensity of the plucking increased. "Oh, I knew I shouldn't have said anything."

"Not at all. I don't mind." Lily put on a pot of water, over the main part of the fire where it would quickly come to a boil. "My parents were down with the fever. The Cherokee call it 'the Important Thing,' because they believe to call its name is to attract its attention. Anyway, a band of Cherokee came through and found them. A lady stayed behind and helped us, but she caught it too and all three died. A couple of the Indians came back, burned all the property to keep anyone else from getting it and took me with them. I was five."

"How awful."

"That water has gone a long way downstream. I can't even remember them. The parents I remember are the Cherokee couple that adopted me, Tall Elk and Sunnua Sweet Cheeks."

Lily removed the chicken, which no longer showed any signs of red, indicating it was getting done. She diced it and added it back to the water where it quickly turned into a presentable chicken stock. A rich aroma wafted across the kitchen. She diced up the prepared vegetables and added them to the pot. She went over to some pots on the windowsill and gathered a little rosemary and some onion, and a couple of other things Carol Sue did not recognize. She chopped them up and added them to the pot, covering it with a lid.

Carol Sue asked cautiously, "But I would think when you got older, you'd want to return to your own people."

"That's just it, *these* are my people." Lily swept her hand to take in the village. "When I go to town, the good citizens look at me as if I am a disgrace. They don't have to say it out loud. I hear their minds saying 'why didn't you kill yourself instead of abandoning your heritage?' Killing oneself is a lot to ask of a five-year-old, wouldn't you say?"

"I certainly would."

"At any rate, the only thing these people have done to me is to love me as if I were one of their own. Whites shun me because I've lived with Indians, but the Cherokee have always treated me as if they saw no difference in us whatsoever. Who is the better Christian?"

"The Cherokee are Christian?" Carol Sue asked.

"A great number of them."

"They're really something, aren't they?"

49

"More than you know," Lily said. "When they came by the house and found my parents ill? They were on their way out of Texas, headed here for the Indian Territory. They were being run out by white men, yet they still had compassion for a white couple and a young girl."

"Why were they being run out?"

"There was a lot of Indian raiding going on out on the western border, so Texas decided to get rid of all of the Indians. They started with those that were the easiest to move, the Cherokee, who had always been their friends."

"How terrible."

"The President of the Texas Republic, Sam Houston, even had a Cherokee wife, yet he allowed it to happen."

Carol Sue looked puzzled, "I don't understand."

"Nor did we. You can see, I ceased to be white a long time ago. I'm Cherokee in every sense of the word and proud of it. I'm even more proud that they consider me to be that as well."

They turned their heads as a scuffling came from the door. The professor said, "May we enter? Are we interrupting?"

"Not at all." She inclined her head. "Enter. My house is honored."

"God bless this house and all who live here," the professor said as they removed their hats and entered. He looked at Carol Sue, "Have you been having a nice visit?"

Carol Sue said, "I've been getting my eyes opened and getting an education to boot."

"Lily is the one who can do that, all right. Quite a remarkable lady."

"Hush your foolish talk and be seated," Lily said. "The food is ready."

They seated themselves, returned the blessing, and began eating quietly, but Carol Sue was still full of questions. She looked at the professor and said, "She's been telling me how she came to be with the Cherokee; it's fascinating. I'm afraid I've been a nuisance, but she's been very patient with me."

"Few can compete with the Cherokee for good manners, young lady, and I'm very familiar with her story. You have much in common."

The professor looked at Lily. "These young people are both orphans too. Carol Sue came to be with me after her parents succumbed to illness, much as yours did. I fear the passing of Bryan's parents was much more difficult. Their wagon train was wiped out by Comanche while he was out hunting. But the result is the same."

Lily shook her head. "The Comanche. They fight so hard to keep their land instead of learning the blessings of sharing."

Bryan frowned. "It sounds like you're defending them."

Lily nodded. "I understand them, which is not the same as approving of their bloodthirsty ways. Look in your Bible in the Old Testament. People were always fighting to take someone else's land, or to keep it. This is not a new thing."

"It says that all right. They used to fight a lot."

"Nothing has changed," the professor said. "People still fight over land. I suppose they always will."

Bryan shook his head slowly. "I never thought of it that way. All we see is them killing and acting terrible. What they see is people trying to take their land."

"There you have it my young friend," the professor said, "the eternal dilemma, blood for land."

Lily said, "It is a shame. My people have been able to learn how to get along without so much bloodshed." She smiled. "But it would seem we do have much in common. For me the solution was as simple as finding where I belong and being with people who love me. That will be the answer for you as well. I wish you luck in finding it."

She looked at them intently. "Yet even if you do not know *where* you belong at this time, I see you at least know *who* you belong with."

Carol Sue smiled, "Yes, the professor came to my aid when I needed it most. I can't say he feels as much like family yet as my parents did." She reached out to take his hand. "But we're growing on one another."

"We are indeed," the professor said. "I admit it's quite a change for an irascible old bachelor like myself to be in lockstep with a beautiful young lady after all these years of living alone, but I must confess that I'm finding having some family to be quite agreeable."

Lily returned Carol Sue's smile. "Feelings for one another are very special and you are being uncommonly wise. They should not be rushed, nor taken lightly. Age is no factor where the heart is involved. The feeling of family will grow as it will."

"It will indeed," The professor said.

Bryan went out to tend the horses and Red Eagle came over to him, leaning on the top rail of the corral, moccasined foot on the bottom rail. Bryan smiled. "What did your uncle think of your outing?"

Red Eagle smiled, "He was pleased."

Bryan finished spreading hay for the horses, picked up a brush, and started to curry one of the animals. "Sounds like you passed the test. How will you know when you're ready?"

"He will say. There will be a ceremony."

"And then you can find out about being a Christian?"

"I think I am ready now. I know of The Great Provider, or God as you call Him." His hand swept the horizon. "I read often in the Bible with my mother, and I know of Jesus. I am ready."

"That's really good." Bryan turned to face Red Eagle. "You do know that's not all there is to it, right?"

"What do you mean?"

Bryan stopped brushing the horse, walked over by Red Eagle, and got very serious. "Just knowing Jesus isn't enough. You have to believe He died to save you from your sins."

Red Eagle nodded solemnly, "I read of this, and believe it is so."

"You have to believe He arose after three days and went to be with His Father in heaven."

"This also do I believe."

Bryan made a gesture of lifting both hands only to let them fall, "Then all that's left is to ask Him to come into your heart and save you from your sins. Do you pray?"

"My mother and I pray often."

"I could help you make the sinner's prayer and help you take the next step," Bryan smiled gently. "But I think it would mean a lot to your mother for you to ask her to pray it with you."

"That's all there is to it?"

Bryan put his hand on his young friend's shoulder. "Most people think it should be much harder than it is, but salvation isn't something we can earn like your tests to become a man. It's a gift from God. All we have to do is ask for it."

"It is good, this gift. I will talk on it with my mother."

"It makes me really happy to have a part in this. Promise me if your mother doesn't want to do this . . . that you'll come back and talk to me."

Red Eagle nodded solemnly again, "This I will do."

The trio didn't overnight in the village, but headed toward Professor Donovan's next stop. They had been on the trail but a couple of hours when the professor pointed into the distance.

"See that bluff ahead? A small creek runs below it and on down to a nice little grove of trees where we shall find a little ranch. It'll really be too early to night camp when we arrive, but I doubt that will matter. People in remote areas such as this get few visitors, so when someone drops by it is always occasion for a social. My life is a steady procession of such events. Not a bad way to live really."

Carol Sue said, "It must be nice to feel so welcome in so many places."

"It certainly is, my dear."

By the time they had made it to the grove the sound of the pots and pans had alerted everyone on the place. They were waiting in the shade of the trees in the yard.

The professor raised a hand and said, "Mr. Thomas, it's good to see you again."

"Now Professor, you know to call me Charley." His good-natured countenance peered out from under the sweat-stained hat. He had a hand hooked into one strap of worn overalls. The other strap was not connected but was somewhere on the inside of the garment. He offered his free hand to the professor to shake.

"I do indeed. And where is the missus?" He looked around for her.

"Sarah is bedridden, Professor. It's getting near her time. Her belly thumps like a ripe watermelon." He laughed.

"Oh my, congratulations are in order. Let's see, this would be . . ."

He counted the four healthy lads standing by the rancher, "number five if my mathematics are in order."

"You ain't counting Carrie. She's the toddler. Two this coming month."

"Tsk, tsk, has it been that long since my last visit?"

"It has for a fact. I'm right glad to see this young lady with you. Mrs. Jorgenson came over to help last time, but she's getting near time herself, so we're on our own this year."

"But I don't know—" Carol Sue stammered.

The professor said, "Hush girl, you don't need to know anything at all about birthing. Sarah has it down pat, but she'll need a lady in there with her to help. You'll do just fine."

"Heavenly days," Carol Sue breathed the words more than saying them.

Introductions were made and they went inside to meet Sarah. She fulfilled her husband's description of ripe to the letter. She was sweating and clearly most uncomfortable. Her dark red hair stuck to her head in ringlets. Carol Sue swung into action, wetting a cloth and moving to wipe Sarah's brow.

The professor said, "Sarah, how is it you can look so lovely under such trying conditions. You look positively radiant."

"Professor, you're an old fraud. I don't look like anything but what I am, fat, hot, and sweaty."

"Not true, not true, but I think perhaps we can help a little. Bryan, will you pull those curtains off her bedside window and take them out to the tank to wet them? Don't wring them out too much so as to leave as much moisture in them as possible. We'll re-hang them and this little breeze will be cooler blowing through them. We'll also take the cooking tarp off the side of the wagon and stretch it up to shade the side of the house. That'll help by a few degrees."

The professor was a man who took charge naturally, "Carol Sue, you're instinctively doing the right thing. You just keep trying to make her as comfortable as you can."

They came out of the house on their mission. Charley fell in with them. The professor stopped. "Charley, there's gonna be a call for a lot of hot water here in a bit, but we don't want to heat up the house by doing it in there. How about you and the boys get a big kettle on and keep it full and bubbling. Mind you do it downwind of the house now; no point in adding to this infernal heat any."

He and Bryan continued their walk to the wagon. The professor whispered. "That ought to give him something meaningful to do and get him out of the way as well."

Bryan grinned, "It ain't gonna be that hard to get me out of the way. This scares me to death."

They stretched the canvas, then everyone got busy with various chores to kill the time. The professor got a rocker and positioned himself under the tarp. Hearing the chair scrape against the wall Sarah said, "Professor, is that you?"

"Yes, Sarah, I'm right here."

She smiled. "Good, I knew you would be."

Carol Sue said, "Here, let me trade your pillow out. You've got that one soaked."

"Thank you. The good Lord was looking out for me when He sent you to me."

"I don't know how much help I'll be. I'm scared."

Sarah settled onto the fresh pillow. It felt cool to her. "My goodness, girl, what do you have to be scared about? I'm the one doing all the work."

"I just don't know what's expected of me."

"We'll help you. There's a reason the professor is outside. He's a mighty knowing man. He knows I can't abide a man in here with me when the baby comes, but if there's a problem, or if I can't tell you what to do, he'll be in here in a shot. And he's been around. He knows what to do: calves, ponies, or human offspring, he knows."

"That's a comfort."

"Yes it is. I have to admit I was feeling a bit alone and sure am . . . ohhh."

"Something wrong?"

Sarah grabbed Carol Sue's hand and gripped hard. Her face registered the pain.

"Professor?"

"Yes, Carol Sue?"

"Something is happening here. She's gripping my hand mighty hard, and her belly is as hard as a rock."

"It's starting then. That's a contraction. You keep hold of that hand and bathe her forehead with that cloth, slow and gentle."

Sarah made primeval, grunting noises.

"Is it coming?"

"Be patient, girl. This may go on for quite a while. You tell me every time her belly gets hard and when it lets up. I'll be timing the contractions."

"All right, she's relaxing."

The professor looked at his watch, noting the time.

The process went on for hours. The interval in between kept getting shorter and shorter.

"Sarah, how are you doing?"

"I think it's about time, Professor."

"You've done this enough, you know better than I when it's time to push. From what Carol Sue says, the baby is positioned right, so when you think it's time, you go."

Sarah took a grip on the head of the bed. "I think it's time to do it." She began to push.

"Talk to us, Carol Sue. Sarah and I need to know what's going on."

"Not much yet, Professor."

"Push again, Sarah, keep pushing. You can do it."

The grunting turned to a scream, loud and sustained.

"The baby is coming, Professor."

It quietened as Sarah caught her breath and gathered herself to continue.

The professor's chair scraped the wall as he leaned forward to listen more closely, "You watch close, girl. You may have to help out a bit."

Sarah took a deep breath, closed her eyes and let it out slowly, then she clenched her fist and gave another big push. The scream filled the room and echoed out over the valley.

Charley and the boys looked up, knowing what it meant.

"How would I help, Professor? Oh, yes, I see . . . there . . . OH-H-H . . . it's coming . . . it's out!"

Sarah's head fell back on the pillow, exhausted.

Outside the window the professor listened with his eyes closed, visualizing what needed to be done. "Fine. You're doing fine. Now take that string I gave you and tie that umbilical cord off on both ends. Tie it nice and tight. Got it? Now cut the cord in between the ties."

"Professor, it's not—"

"Don't fret, girl, grab that youngun by the ankles and hold it upside down and give it a nice solid smack."

There was the sound of a crisp *smack*, followed by an angry cry that increased in volume until it matched the sound Sarah had made earlier.

"There," he laughed, leaning back in his chair again, "you just needed to give that baby the proper welcome to the world. Wipe it off quickly, and get it in that nice warm blanket."

"It's a girl. She's beautiful. Her bottom lip is trembling."

"She's very angry with us right now. Hand her to her mother, and let them get acquainted. Congratulations, Sarah. Sounds like you did very well."

"I sure am glad you two were here." She looked down as Carol Sue placed the small bundle in her arms. "Oh, she's beautiful."

"Is it safe to look in now?"

"Of course, look at her."

The professor got up and leaned on the window sill to look in.

"Sarah, you have indeed done yourself proud."

"I'm grateful Carol Sue was here, and you too."

"I'm honored to have been here, Sarah. Purely honored. Carol Sue, when she's ready, Sarah is going to tell you how to clean her up and finish things up. I'm gonna go tell Charley he's a daddy and see if I don't have a cigar or two in my stock. I'll have him bring a pan of that hot water for you to use cleaning up." He winked. "Since I had him heat it, we best use some of it. Right, Sarah?"

As he walked away Sarah said, "Men, you'd think the way they carry on that it was them having the baby."

12

They named their daughter Crystal Ann, immediately launching into a celebration with a barbecue and a fine party. The professor and his two young companions stayed for several days until Sarah was back on her feet and had regained her strength.

"I sure hate to see you go," Sarah stood by the wagon where they were packed and ready to leave. "It was nice to have another woman around for a while."

"A woman," Carol Sue beamed. "You know, I don't think I've ever been called that before."

"You handled yourself as one. Besides, in the west it isn't a matter of age. I was younger than you when I had my first."

"No kidding?"

The professor nodded. "Yes, it's a hard country, and young people tend to grow up fast. You're seeing it for yourself firsthand."

"Yes," Bryan said, "I've grown more in the past few months than in the whole rest of my life."

"Well, until the next time, my friends." The professor whipped up his team and they pulled out.

"Don't forget the way back," Charley shouted. "You're always welcome."

★   ★   ★

Bryan looked at the girl on the wagon seat above him. *Something is different. She's different. Maybe there is something to this stuff about her turning into a woman.*

She noticed him looking and smiled.

He returned the smile, "You act like you're a hunnert miles away."

"Me? I'm sorry. Woolgathering, I guess. That was such a wonderful experience, seeing that new life birthed. I don't know how to tell you. It was a miracle. It did something to me."

"I know; I can see it. You actually look different."

"Do I?"

The professor chuckled, "What you're seeing is maturity, Bryan. Carol Sue grew up a little back there. Having a part in a birth is as close as you can come to interfacing with God himself. It's like being in on the act of creation."

"Yes! That's it," Carol's face was radiant. "I felt like I got the chance to do something totally amazing."

"You did. And I know what you've been so quiet about. I know what's on your mind."

"You think so?" She raised her chin, "You men think you know everything."

"Ah no, I told you earlier the more I learned the more I realized there was yet to learn. High on the list of things I don't know is how to understand the fair sex, but in this case I believe I do know. You're thinking that someday it'll be you bringing that new life into the world."

"How did you know that?" She looked at him with wonder on her face.

"It's written all over you. If you think it was a miracle helping, wait until you see how it feels to be the one doing it."

"Sarah didn't seem to have much fun. I could tell it really hurt."

"Sure it hurt," he said softly. "Did you ask her if it was worth it?"

"No, I didn't have to. I could see it was, and she's done it six times. She did say the pain was the price she had to pay to get to be a mother."

The professor had a small smile. "That's how it looks to me. It's part of the bonding process. It ties the mother and child together forever."

"Forever," she said softly.

The professor raised an eyebrow, "Something wrong?"

"I don't know that I'm ready for what she just went through. And I sure don't know that I'm ready for forever."

The professor smiled. "Forever is a long enough time that you don't have to be in a hurry to get there. It's good you're thinking about the future instead of rushing toward it, but don't be in a hurry to get it all planned out. What is meant to be will happen. By the time you find yourself someone, you'll see it different. You see, darlin', the missing ingredient is love."

"I see."

He turned the team into a little shady area. "Here we are."

"Here we are where?" Bryan said.

"This is a little spot where ground ivy grows prolifically. I use it in making my stomach medicine."

Bryan shook his head. "I've been meaning to talk to you about that, Professor. I ain't partial to taking part in no snake oil show."

"I'd never consider it either, Bryan. I thought I told you that. The medicine I produce is legitimate concoctions based on herbs and natural healing. Did I mention I'm writing a book on the subject?"

"No."

"I am. It has little drawings of the plants, where they can be found, and the uses of each. Unlike the medicine show-man that you are so concerned about, I do not have one cure-all ointment, but a number of carefully researched cures, individually bottled."

"No kidding?"

"Not a bit. I don't sell them in a public performance and generally not to the public at all. I market them through general stores and merchants, plus they are purchased and stocked by most of the physicians around the area. I produce different medicines when I am at the place where the ingredients may be found."

"Well, I'll be. You mean they're real medicines?"

"They are," the professor said. "Just because they aren't produced in some laboratory back east doesn't lessen the medicinal value any. It's hard to get stocks of those products out here. I produce many of the same products, in much smaller quantities, of course."

"Well, my goodness."

Professor Donovan looked at his traveling companions. He could tell his stock had just gone up significantly with Bryan. They got down, tied off the horses, and he handed them a couple of baskets.

"If you two will assist me by filling these with these green, round leaves," he showed them exactly the leaves he wanted, "we'll set up production after we eat."

"You make money with this?"

"In truth, yes. My traveling merchandise sales are a modest income, but more of a service to my friends along the way. My main income is producing and distributing my medicines. And that's where I derive my primary satisfaction."

They set up camp, and while Carol Sue prepared the meal, Bryan and the professor put the leaves on to boil in creek water. "Different preparations are required to release the medicinal effect in various plants and herbs. In this case, water is all that's necessary. While I'm preparing it, you could assist me in making the containers ready."

He set Bryan to work pasting printed labels on a batch of bottles. The label read *Professor Donovan's Stomach Tonic.* Smaller print proclaimed it would *ease gripping pains, gas and choleric conditions of the stomach and spleen. Use to treat*

Yellow Jaundice, melancholy, to release urine, and to treat women's complaints.

"This really works?"

"Quite well actually."

"They look like big-time patent medicines."

"They should. I have a printer in St. Louis that prepares all my labels for me."

After they ate, they poured the medication into the bottles, sealing the stoppers with hot wax.

"Tomorrow we'll gather some black haw and make my fever tonic. It uses alcohol as a solvent, so I'll have to set up my little still tonight and let it begin distilling spirits. I have some sour mash in that barrel that we'll use in that process."

He got his book, and they looked at it. "Here's what the plant looks like." The writing by the illustration showed the plant to be beneficial in the treatment of chills and fever and in treating palpitation of the heart.

"Did I mention that I have quite a number of medical doctors on my client list?"

"Yes." Bryan nodded somberly. "That's pretty impressive."

Carol Sue said, "Professor, I see in this book where this is supposed to be *an invaluable treatment for mothers who are subject to miscarriage.*"

"Yes, it is effective there and helps arrest bleeding following delivery."

"I had no idea. I mean, before you told us about this, I was like Bryan. I thought—"

"Yes, I know. The itinerant medicine showpeople are a major thorn in my side. But I've spent much of my life tracing down and documenting these herb and plant uses and cures. I have quite a collection of letters attesting to the success of the preparations that I bring out now and then, if the local constabulary mistakes me for a charlatan."

Bryan said, "Well, I feel like I owe you an apology."

"Not at all, my friend. Quite natural. Now it will be necessary for us to take turns tending the fire under the still tonight, and we shall have to insure that there is water in the kettle part of it so it won't boil dry."

13

Several days later the trio rode into the little town of Turkey Creek. "I have two clients here, Dr. Thompson and Ralph Jessup over at the general store. The doctor is a straight sale, but my transaction with Ralph will entail dickering for merchandise, I fear."

"Is there a sheriff?" Bryan's voice sounded nervous.

"Sheriff Jack Treadwell. I know what you have in mind. I recommend that you wait until I transact my business so I may assist you."

"All right by me. A little support wouldn't hurt my feelings none."

"In the interim why don't you check us into a hotel room—my treat. Bryan and I will share a room and of course separate accommodations are in order for you, my dear."

"Oh my," Carol said, "a real bed. It's been such a long time."

"A luxury I like to permit myself whenever possible, and the dining room provides excellent fare."

The professor found them waiting in chairs on the hotel porch a couple of hours later. Bryan said, "How'd it go?"

"Splendid, just splendid. They were quite low on stock. Are you ready?"

"Not really," Bryan said as he reluctantly got up, "but I got it to do."

"I'm not sure it's even necessary, but I can see it will relieve your mind."

They walked down the street to the sheriff's office. The occupant was asleep with his feet on the desk, his hat over his eyes. He wasn't a young man, had gray in his temples and mustache and a potbelly lapping over his belt.

"A-hemmmm."

"What . . . what . . ." The feet came down with a thump. "Oh, it's you, Professor. When did you get into town?"

"A few hours ago. We have a little business to transact with you."

"A little business?" He buttoned, then straightened his vest and pulled his hat down correctly. "Don't you go getting the wrong idea. I'm often up half the night. This job can have some long hours."

"Tut, tut, Sheriff, I'd never begrudge a man a well-earned nap. Everyone well appreciates the fine job you do for them."

"Well, as long as you recognize . . . and by the way, that bottle you gave me last trip for my arthritis has really done the trick."

"I'm pleased it worked." The professor held up another bottle. "I thought you might be out of it, so I brought you another one."

"I surely am out." He pulled out a worn coin purse and began peering into it.

"Put your money away, Sheriff. It's the least I can do for a dedicated public servant."

The sheriff looked relieved as he snapped it closed. "Well, that's right nice of you. You said something about some business?"

"The business would be mine," Bryan said. "I left a horse over at the livery stable. I'd appreciate it if you would turn it over to its owner when he comes to town."

"What's this owner's name?"

"I don't know his last name; he went by Fat Jack. After my folks were killed when Indians attacked our wagon train I ran into him. He had a captive Cherokee girl that he was treating badly, and he made me stay with him as well. He beat me quite a bit. When me and the girl run off, I took his horse so he couldn't run us down, but I wasn't stealing it. I just had to have time to get away. That's why I'm turning it in to you, to make that clear."

The lawman listened somberly. When Bryan finished, the sheriff scratched his head and said, "Yeah, a couple of cowboys found the body. I'm afraid them Injun's was mighty hard on him. He ain't gonna be needing that horse."

Bryan grimaced, "I was afraid of that, but I don't know what else I could have done."

"Surely you can see he had nothing to do with the man's death, Sheriff," the professor said.

"Well, leaving a man afoot in Injun territory ain't much different than shooting him, but I reckon the law don't see it that way. Legally I reckon I couldn't charge him with murder."

"I'm very glad to hear that."

"There is the little matter of being a horse thief though. That's a hanging offense in these parts."

"Sheriff! You know he wasn't stealing the horse, you heard him say he was just taking it to prevent Fat Jack from coming after either of them."

"I'd like to say that makes a difference, Professor. I really would, but its outta my hands now. I got to hold him for the judge and wire the federal marshal."

The professor frowned, "This is most exasperating." He looked at the youngsters, "I shouldn't have dawdled so. I should have come here directly, then doubled back to make my stops."

"I won't lock 'em up or nuthin, Professor. I'll release them into your charge. The judge is gonna hold a trial when the marshal gets here, and he's due in a couple of days. He's coming to hang a horse thief I got back in the cellblock." He looked at Bryan. "That's why I have to make sure this case is heard too. Wouldn't look right to try one and just let the other off. It's up to the judge to decide, not me."

"Surely you mean they are going to try a man or men *suspected* of stealing a horse."

"Well, that too."

"Has the man representation?"

"We ain't got no lawyers here."

"Then for what it is worth, I shall be representing my young friends in court. I might talk to this man as well. May I see him?"

Judge O'Dell was a spare man, short in stature, with wire rimmed glasses and no chin at all. He looked more like a bookworm than a pillar of jurisprudence. United States Marshal Jeremiah Spade on the other hand, was a hawk, a predator. He glowered at the judge at the table serving as the judge's bench situated on a riser in the corner of the saloon, which was closed for the proceedings. Spade was big, but not fat, and peered out from under bushy eyebrows whose gray matched that in his pork-chop sideburns and flowing mustache.

"Order in the court," the judge yelled, banging on the table with a bung-starter obtained from the bartender. "You people sit down."

There was a good crowd in the courtroom owing to the scarcity of entertainment in the little town.

"Let's go ahead and tend to the hanging first and get it out of the way." The judge looked over his spectacles.

The professor jumped to his feet, "I object most strenuously."

"And who might you be?"

"I am Professor Harold Donovan. I'm not licensed to practice before the bar, but in the absence of a practicing barrister, I'm prepared to argue for the defendant. In this case, and in the next case to follow."

"You do sound like a confounded lawyer."

"I am not without experience, licensed to practice or not."

"Just what I need, a wannabe lawyer. State your objection, counselor."

"I object to the phrase *getting on with the hanging*, your honor" the professor said, "Unless I woke up in a foreign country this morning, the defendant is innocent until proven guilty."

"Are you sure you aren't a lawyer?"

"A lot of my friends at Harvard read for the law. We discussed it a lot."

"You went to Harvard?"

"Graduated in '47, your honor. Received my masters in '48 and my doctorate a year and a half later."

"Doctor? Doctor of what?"

"Doctor of Letters, your honor," the professor lifted his chin and grasped his coat lapel with his left hand, unable to resist a small show of pride.

"Literary. I might have known." A look came over the judge's face as if he had just bit into something distasteful. "Why do you call yourself professor instead of doctor?"

"It's a title others have placed upon me. West of the Mississippi people pretty much associate the word doctor with medical doctor. I don't wish to mislead anyone, particularly since I traffic in the practice of pharmaceuticals."

"I see. Very well, I grant the fact that the *accused* is on trial for horse stealing. Jackson, did you steal that horse?"

"Objection, your honor," the professor said.

"Now what?"

"Are you not going to ask how the defendant pleads?"

"Pleads for his life, I imagine. What's your point, counselor?"

"The defendant pleads innocent, your honor, by reason of mitigating circumstances."

The judge let out a long ragged breath and looked at the ceiling. "Next thing I know you're gonna be wanting a jury trial."

"Without a doubt, your honor."

"And if I say no?"

"I furnish the governor with his lumbago medicine, your honor, and the attorney general swears by my stomach tonic. I doubt that I'd have trouble getting an audience with them."

Addressing the ceiling again, the judge said, "Why me? Very well, counselor, will those in the saloon . . . er . . . the courtroom do, or do you wish to send to the statehouse for jurors in order for them to be unbiased?"

"I trust the people in this community implicitly, your honor."

"That's a relief," the judge sighed deeply.

The jury selection took a couple of hours. Then the court was adjourned until the following morning as the crowd was beginning to get a bit unruly.

14

The judge rapped the gavel. "I suppose you will be prosecuting for the state, Marshal Spade?"

"That's the usual procedure when there ain't no lawyers and the state ain't sent nobody." The lawman seemed short on patience.

"Very well, you are ready to proceed?"

The marshal had his chair rocked back on the rear legs. He reeked of boredom. "I was ready yesterday. I got a couple of fugitive warrants to go serve. I ain't got time for this foolishness."

The judge's voice was clipped. "You have as much time as I say it takes, Marshal. Don't go trying to bully me. Even a marshal may be placed in jail for contempt of court."

"I'd like to see you try that." The look he gave the judge fell nothing short of pure intimidation.

"Keep it up, Marshal, you'll get the chance to see close at hand."

Bryan heard Sheriff Treadwell speak under his breath, "Oh, man, don't make me try to throw that brush panther into my hoosegow. He's tougher than a wagon load of horse-shoe nails." Sweat poured from Treadwell's face.

The judge looked at the professor. "Is the defense ready?"

The professor stood, "We are, your honor."

"Proceed, Marshal, bring your charges."

"This here thing is open and shut, your honor. Clem McDonough and Slim Edgar caught Smitty there riding one of their horses. Caught him big as life. They're prepared to swear to it."

"Marshal, is this your first trial? You're supposed to stand when you address the court."

Spade made no move, but raised the right side of his upper lip as he looked at the judge through hooded eyes.

"Call your witnesses."

Still without rising Spade said, "I call Clem McDonough."

Clem was sworn in and did swear to the facts just as the marshal had presented them. The professor closed on him.

"Clem, you're a hand on the Lazy J Ranch?"

Clem nodded, "Everybody knows that."

"Judge, would you instruct the witness he is just to answer my questions yes or no?"

"You heard him, Clem."

"Yes."

The professor continued, "You ever have a horse that played out on you while you were way out on the range?"

"Every cowboy has had that happen."

"Judge?"

"I'm not going to tell you again to answer yes or no."

"Yes."

"How did you get back?"

"Ain't no way to answer that yes or no."

The judge's frustration was beginning to show, "Then just answer the man."

"I'd find one at some ranch or something and borrow him to get home."

The professor threw up his hands, "Your honor, this witness is confessing to horse theft."

Clem jumped to his feet. "I ain't doing no such thing! Judge, I just borrowed a horse long enough to get into town. I returned him. Everybody has done that from time to time."

The judge used the gavel like a pile driver, "Sit down, Clem, and address yourself to the lawyer . . . er . . . to the professor . . . aw, you know what I mean."

"Clem," the professor said quietly, "did Smitty tell you that was what he was doing with the horse he was riding?"

"Sure he did, but we knew better. He was headed in the opposite direction from town."

"What direction would that be?"

"South."

"Excuse the witness," the professor said, "I won't press the horse stealing charges against him."

"Ain't no charges to press," Clem mumbled as he returned to his seat.

The marshal called Slim to the stand and elicited his testimony. Then he turned him over to the professor.

Before he could even open his mouth, the cowboy said, "Your tricks won't do no good on me, I ain't never borrowed no horse no time."

"I see, that's admirable. Have any of your friends had to do that?"

"Well, from time to time."

"Did you hang them?"

"Hang them? Are you kidding? They took the horses back."

"As Smitty would have done had he been allowed to do so."

"Clem done told you he was riding away from town, not towards it."

"Pass the witness."

Slim went back to his seat and said loudly enough for the courtroom to hear, "Guess I showed him."

"Marshal?" the judge asked.

"Prosecution rests, your honor, and can we go ahead and hang him today? I really do have to get going."

The judge looked at the professor. "You got anything else?"

"The defense calls Macdonald Kirby."

The rancher came to the stand and was sworn in.

The professor came to stand in front of him, "Mr. Kirby, you run a ranch outside of town?"

"I do."

"Where is it located?"

"Just south of the Lazy J."

The professor looked off in that direction, "South? How far south?"

"We share a creek with them. We both use it to water stock."

"So that would be the south boundary of the Lazy J?"

"It would, and my north boundary."

The professor acted as if he didn't understand, "Are you saying that it would be *much* closer from the Lazy J to your place than to town?"

"By quite a few miles."

The professor leaned in close, "Mr. Kirby, do you sell horses?"

"I do."

"Who else does?"

"Swanson, over at the livery stable. A couple of other ranches."

"They have pretty good prices?"

"Swanson is high as the dickens. Most of the ranches are pretty fair."

"I object," a voice yelled.

"Shut up, Swanson," the judge banged his gavel. "You have no legal standing here. Besides, you know it's the gospel truth. That matched pair you sold me for my carriage cost me double what it should have."

The professor stifled a snicker, "Now that's settled, Mr. Kirby. If you were going to buy a horse, where would you go?"

The rancher smiled. "I see where you're going with this. Nobody in their right mind would ride out of their way to go spend extra money for a horse."

"You think Smitty was headed to your place? He said he was."

"He'd have to be crazy to not be heading to my place."

"Your honor, the defense rests."

It only took the jury ten minutes to acquit the cowboy. The court turned its attention to Bryan.

The professor kicked it off, "Your honor, in the matter of the theft against the person of Fat Jack Wallace, the defendant wishes to enter a plea of self-defense."

"I'm not even sure self-defense is an appropriate plea on a theft charge. I never heard of such a thing."

"I believe I can substantiate it, your honor."

"Counselor, you done wore me clear out. We gonna go through this whole trial again?"

The professor nodded, "We want a jury trial, your honor."

"I guess this jury won't do?"

"There is a different set of questions I'd like to use in seating a new jury, your honor."

The judge sat there for several minutes looking glum. Suddenly he brightened up. "We're skipping a step here. I need to look at the evidence and see if the defendant needs to be bound over for trial."

"That's acceptable, your honor."

The judge pointed at Bryan with the handle of his gavel, "Young man, you're the one that done it. Get up here on the stand and tell your story."

Bryan took the stand.

The professor stood there a moment, then said, "Did you pay close attention to the preceding trial?"

"I sure did, particularly since we're facing the same charges."

"Is there anything different about your situation than that one?"

Bryan nodded. "I didn't want or need the horse. I just had to get it out of his reach to let that young Comanche girl have time to get away from him. He was abusing her something terrible, and I just couldn't let that stand."

"So you took the horse not to steal it, but to rescue the girl. Why didn't you just take it off a ways and let it go?"

"It would have probably just gone back to him, and we'd have been in for it then."

The professor put a hand on his forehead. "Can you be more specific about what you mean by the phrase *in for it*?"

"He said if I crossed him that he'd kill me."

The professor turned to face the judge, "Are you saying you took the horse in defense of your life?"

"A boy like me couldn't have stopped him from killing me if he set his mind to it."

The professor turned back to Bryan, "Yet you had the chance to kill him?"

"Sure. In fact after I laid him out with that skillet, the Indian girl would have killed him with his own knife if I hadn't stopped her."

"In spite of the fact that you were in fear of your own life you saved his life?"

"It was the right thing to do."

"If you couldn't set the horse free, what did you intend to do with it?"

"Exactly what I did. I took it to the nearest town, which is here. I put it at the livery stable and notified the sheriff where it was if Fat Jack came looking for it."

"But he isn't going to come looking for it, is he?"

Bryan looked down and shook his head, "Not from what the sheriff said. He said they had found his body."

"That wasn't what you intended?"

The look of sincere regret was clear on his face. "If that had been what I wanted, I could have done it while he was knocked out."

"It sounds to me like you are guilty of rescuing a young lady being abused and delivering the horse to the closest constituted authority."

There was a murmuring in the courtroom. Western men didn't hold with abusing womenfolk, and the phrase about the abuse didn't set well with them.

The judge looked across the courtroom. "Marshal, are you acquainted with the victim?"

"I've got a fugitive warrant on him, your honor, murder and robbery. He's one of those I was after."

"And if you'd caught up with him?"

"I'd probably had to kill him. He was the type."

"Young man, whether you intended his death to be the result of your actions or not, it appears you have saved us considerable time and expense. The court finds there is not sufficient evidence to hold you over for trial. In fact, I further find that you should be commended for your actions rather than censored."

"Your honor?"

"Yes, Marshal?"

"It's more than that," the marshal said. "Like I said, I was after Fat Jack, and according to that fugitive warrant he had a $3,000 reward on his head, dead or alive. If you are ruling the way you are, don't that mean the young man is entitled to the reward?"

"He is indeed. Court dismissed. Sheriff Treadwell, please see to the distribution of the reward."

After the trial Bryan went to the Western Union office. He sent messages to the families of the people from the wagon train. He wired money to those he had addresses for. He came back to the hotel to find Carol Sue and the professor up in the room.

"I sure feel better about getting that done," Bryan said.

The professor shook his head, "I suppose you know if Fat Jack had known you were carrying all that money, he'd have killed you for sure."

"It was right under his nose the whole time."

"Did it leave you with anything?" the professor asked.

"I have my pa's money and that from a couple of people I had no relatives addresses for. One of them had a substantial cash box. As far as I'm concerned, you two are partners in it now too, Professor, and there's the reward to consider too."

"You know, that's not a bad idea," the professor said. "I don't have any relatives either other than Carol Sue. I'll draw up some papers, and we'll just have us a three way split on my enterprises as well. I don't have anybody else to leave it to."

Bryan said, "That's not what I meant."

"I know it wasn't, but if we're going to be partners, we have to be partners all the way."

They counted the money he had remaining. It came to $3,226.50 including the proceeds from Fat Jack's belongings. The reward was going to nearly double that amount.

"Six thousand dollars," Bryan said. "You know how long it would take a forty dollar a month cowhand to make that?"

"I think you intend that as a rhetorical question, but if you didn't, the answer is nearly twelve and a half years. But we had best get over to the bank and put it on deposit and see if the reward money is ready to be put there as well."

"We'll just have to pull it out when we leave."

"No, that's the beauty of it. We can simply deposit it and get a bank draft. Any bank will cash it, or we can get a portion of it and a new draft for the balance. It's much better than carrying a lot of cash. I have better than $4,000 in bank drafts in my possession now. You now own a share of that, plus my inventory and the patents on my medical processes."

"This doesn't seem right," Bryan said. "You've worked all your life to get where you are."

"Yet it would appear you are bringing as much to the operation as I am, even more. In fact, it appears our little enterprise is very well capitalized. We'll have to give this some thought as to where we go from here."

"It sure gives us something different to think about."

15

"The thing is, this partnership serves another useful purpose," the professor said. "Even though we are related, having another person traveling with us very much helps with the appearance of our situation. I don't want people getting the wrong idea about a young lady traveling with me."

"You figure that to be a problem?"

"Fat Jack probably would have said that Indian girl was his ward, but it surely wasn't a real relationship. I don't want even the slightest appearance of impropriety."

"Whatever that is."

"It is rather ironic though, don't you think?" The professor smiled. "Usually it would be someone my age chaperoning the two of you, yet it seems we shall do the opposite."

"What does that mean?"

"What?"

"Ironic."

"Irony is the incongruity between what might be expected and what actually occurs."

Bryan's shoulders fell. "Can't you get closer to it than that? I never saw anybody before that was such hard work to talk to."

"It means something sounds the opposite of how it ought to be."

"How about chaperone?"

"It means have somebody with you to make sure things are above board at all times."

"I get it. I can see how you wouldn't want anybody to get the wrong idea about her traveling with you."

"Very sensible. Well, we get along nicely, and I have surely enjoyed the company. And since we are planning a business venture together, it just makes good sense to be traveling companions."

"Excuse me," a man said, "I'm sorry to intrude in your conversation, but did you say this young lady is traveling with two unattached males?"

The professor looked at him. "We are traveling companions, yes." The professor stepped forward and extended his hand. "I'm Harold Donovan, and this is Bryan Wheeler and Carol Sue Finney. She is my ward."

"Yes, Mr. Donovan, or perhaps I should say Professor Donovan, I know who you are. I witnessed your remarkable performance in court. I also became acquainted with these young people in that context. I am on the board of supervisors for the orphanage outside of town, and in that capacity I'm afraid I came away from that event with a concern." He turned to look at Bryan, "How old are you, son?"

"About to turn seventeen."

"And you, young lady?"

"Nearly sixteen."

The professor got the drift of where the questions were heading, "Don't get the wrong idea. I've been traveling with these young people and all concerned are conducting themselves in a most appropriate manner. There has been no intimacy involved between anyone, and to further the propriety of the matter is why we are all desiring to travel with a proper chaperone."

"I'm pleased to hear that," the man said, "but I don't think they are old enough to fully know their mind on the subject. I could not in all conscience allow an impressionable young lady to go off on the trail with two single males such as the two of you."

"And just exactly what makes you think you have any say on the subject?"

The man stiffened his backbone, "Mister Donovan, I am not accustomed to people taking that tone with me."

"And I, sir, am not accustomed to dealing with such a sanctimonious hypocrite."

"Well, I never . . ."

"Obviously."

The professor spun on his heel and taking Carol Sue by the hand, stormed out the door. Bryan followed in confusion. On the way out the professor said, "Let's get out of here; I think we've pretty much wore out our welcome."

Carol Sue said, "I don't understand what happened."

"He's a bigot is what happened, but I shouldn't have let him get under my skin that way. I'm afraid I don't suffer fools well."

Bryan said, "Well, like Fat Jack used to say, you sure buck quick."

"Yes . . . yes . . . I'll not deny it. Listen, Ralph should have our provisions assembled by now. Let's pick them up and be on our way. I find the hospitality of this community sadly lacking."

They made their way to the store and were busy loading their supplies when the prune-faced man from the orphanage walked up. With him were Sheriff Treadwell and Judge O'Dell. He said, "There she is, Sheriff. Do your duty."

"What's this all about?" The professor stepped in front of Carol Sue.

"Mr. Sexton has lodged a complaint. Seems he thinks you two have a minor female in your possession, and he thinks it ain't seemly."

"Sheriff, judge, you know this young lady is legally in my care in spite of what that uppity fellow is saying."

"Nothing uppity about it. It simply isn't right." The man looked out from the safety of standing behind the big lawman.

"Don't listen to him. He's just mad because I called his hand on it. I shouldn't have, I know, and he probably wouldn't be doing this if I hadn't angered him. It's my fault."

The judge said, "Well, all the same, he is quite correct. The young lady is a minor, and she is an orphan. I see no difference between this situation and the one you argued so eloquently about in court. It will be necessary for us to place her in a home until I decide the disposition of the case."

"A home? With a family? She is already in the legal care of the only family she has remaining."

"Actually, it will need to be at the orphanage."

"What?" Bryan yelled.

"Oh no!" Carol Sue said.

"Judge, you can't do this," the professor said. "The orphanage is for children, kids who cannot take care of themselves. Miss Finney is a young woman legally in my care. To do as you propose would be preposterous."

"I can and I must. Sheriff, take charge of the young lady please. You will need to take her to your office until someone arrives from the orphanage to take charge of her."

The pair watched them walk off with her. She looked back at them with tears in her eyes.

"This is all my fault," the professor said.

The two pulled up some distance out of town, Bryan riding beside the wagon. "This is some fine kettle of fish," Bryan lamented. "Now what are we going to do?"

"I've been thinking on the problem. We have to analyze it in a logical fashion. There will be no hearing on the subject in the near future if at all, and we can't just wait around for her to come of age, so legal action is out of the question. I don't propose to try and take her from the sheriff, so seeming to leave town was our best primary maneuver."

"Glad to hear you say it was just a maneuver," Bryan said. "I was worried that we were really leaving her. To tell you the truth, if that was the case, we were fixing to part company."

"Don't be silly. I'd never go off and leave her this way. She's the only family I have."

"I'm relieved to hear it, so like I said, what do we do?"

"Well, I just said what I feel we *can't* do. It seems to me that our best option will be available when the representative from the orphanage comes to collect her. Those places are no toriously understaffed, so it is very unlikely that there wi'' more than one. The sheriff might ride escort, but I do he will go the entire way. If he decides to deliver he to come up with something else."

"You're planning on taking her?"

The professor grinned, "Actually, g on *you* tak-ing her."

"You don't have the backbor ?"

The professor shook his he isn't that. After you do it, you'll have to go on the ru I can't run expeditiously in a wagon with all this gear, so I´ll be easy to catch up to. I plan on saying you were mad at me after my foolish talk brought this on, and we split up. That wouldn't be all that far from the truth."

"Where will we go?"

"I don't know, or wish to know. I'll write down my itiner-ary, so you can meet up with me after a bit. You have the bank drafts, so money won't be a problem. I think you'll do fine, and I know you will keep her safe until we get back together. We'll discuss our new business plans then."

Bryan was clearly downhearted. "That doesn't sound like much of a plan."

"No, granted it is not. It does seem the best I can do under the circumstances, however. Do you have any better ideas?"

"No, I guess not. I better get me a kerchief to wear as a mask and go over where I can watch the trail."

"Yes, a mask is a good idea, though I doubt it will fool anyone."

★   ★   ★

It was almost too easy. Just before sunset a surrey came by with Carol Sue and a pickle-faced lady in a severe black dress. There was no outrider. Bryan rode out in front and waved the big pistol he had taken from Fat Jack. "Stand and deliver," he shouted.

"Young man," pickle face said, "what do you think you are doing?"

"I'm sticking you up, that's what I'm doing."

"I'm carrying nothing of value."

"I ain't after your money."

"Now look here, I can't allow—"

"Ain't up to you. Carol Sue, you climb down from there and get your things. Your horse is right behind that brush. I'll just stay here and keep Miss Pickle Face company."

"Now you see here—"

"Ma'am, I'm a peaceable man by nature. Don't make me shoot you. It'd ruin my whole day."

"Well, it wouldn't do much for mine either."

"Bryan," Carol Sue called from the brush. "I'm ready."

"Okay, you come out here and hold this gun on her. I'm gonna cut that doubletree loose and let those horses go."

"You wouldn't leave me here stranded."

"Actually I seem to be making a career of it. You're my third in just a couple of months." He chuckled. "Don't worry, you won't be here long. Those horses will light a shuck for the barn. Soon as they see them come in with all the harness still on them, they'll come looking. It oughta give us a couple hours head start though, especially adding in the time it'll take to fetch the sheriff. I reckon that'll be plenty."

Bryan gave the horses a swat on the rump, and they headed out at a trot toward their home barn. Bryan swung up on his horse, tipped his hat to the lady and said, "A good evening to you, ma'am. Sorry to have to inconvenience you this way, but then none of this needed happen in the first place."

After they had gotten out of site of the hapless lady sitting in the surrey, Carol Sue said, "Where's the professor?"

"He figures the posse is going to be able to track him right easy. He headed in the opposite direction. I've got a list of all the places he's headed though and we can catch back up when it's safe. But for now, it's just us."

They stopped to retrieve the packhorse with all their belongings. Then they rode off into the night.

"Full moon rising," Bryan pointed out, "Be easy to see. I think it'd be smart for us to just ride through the night. We can always catch up on our sleep later."

16

It wasn't until the following morning that a hired hand at the orphanage discovered horses in the barn with harness still on them. His first reaction was anger that someone had come in and left them in that condition. It wasn't until he noticed the surrey had not returned with the horses that it occurred to him to worry.

He backtracked to town, leading the team until he found pickle face stranded in the wagon. She was lying across the seat in a most uncomfortable-looking position, but she was asleep.

"Miss Fawcett?"

She came awake and sat upright in a single motion. She fought to get awake. "Mr. Blackshear, have I been here all night?"

"I reckon so, ma'am. I didn't find these here horses in the barn until morning chores. What happened? The hitch pin break on you?"

She straightened the austere little hat on her head and tried to compose herself. "It most certainly did not, and I simply cannot believe you left me here all night."

"Ain't my fault. I had no way of knowing I needed to go check the barn."

He backed the horses up to the wagon and connected the doubletree. "It don't seem right bringing them back without them even having the rigging off, but I guess they got rest enough even with it. Didn't make any sense taking it off and putting it right back on either."

Pickle face was not to be placated. As soon as he completed hooking them up, he handed her the reins, and she whipped up the team immediately, turning in a tight circle and almost running over his foot. She was not sparing with the buggy whip as she disappeared down the road back to town.

Blackshear rubbed the back of his neck as he stood there watching. "Silly woman. No *thanks for coming to get me*, or kiss my foot, or anything. Now I know why I ain't ever felt the need to get hitched to no female."

He remounted and headed back to the orphanage, shaking his head.

Miss Fawcett hit town at a dead run. She leaned back into the reins and set the brake as she came to the sheriff's office. The horses slid to a stop, and the wagon slid sideways sending dirt clods all over the sidewalk at the feet of the grocer who had spent the last thirty minutes sweeping it off. He was less than pleased.

She jumped from the wagon and ran into the sheriff's office in a most unladylike manner. The door slammed back against the wall causing the deputy napping with his feet on the desk to go over backwards.

"What the tarnation!" He peeked gingerly over the desk expecting to find a Comanche war party at the very least. Instead he found one very disheveled-looking female, but she WAS in full battle array.

"You!" She pinned him to the wall with her gaze. "Where is the sheriff?"

"He's taking breakfast over at the hotel."

Without another word she spun and stomped across the street. A number of spectators had already been lured out by the commotion. The grocer, dirt clods on his shoes, still had not moved.

Sheriff Treadwell had just placed a bite of biscuit and gravy in his mouth when she screeched at him like a diving falcon. "Sheriff!"

Startled, he choked on the bite, started turning red and fought for air that would not come.

"Are you listening to me?"

She hit him upside the head with her purse, which mercifully dislodged the obstruction in his throat. He collapsed in his chair.

Her face suddenly thrust within an inch of his own. "Are you deaf?"

"Madam, have you taken leave of your senses?"

He retrieved the napkin from the table and mopped the sweat and gravy from his face. He took a sip of water to ease his throat.

"You nearly killed me."

"I did nothing to you at all, but those brigands have kidnapped the young lady you placed in my charge yesterday."

"When did this happen?" His senses were beginning to return.

"Last night."

"Why did you wait until now to tell me about it?"

"It wasn't my idea. They set the horses free. I was stranded out in the wilderness all night long."

"Wilderness, my foot. It ain't but a few miles out to the orphanage. It's practically in town. Why didn't you just walk out or back, one or the other."

"Surely you jest."

"What's going on here?" Treadwell spun to see Judge O'Dell approaching. The situation was deteriorating rapidly for the sheriff.

"Hello, Judge, your sister-in-law was just telling me that girl you sent her to the orphanage with has been kidnapped."

"How long ago?"

"Hello, Stanford, about time someone with some reason was involved in this. She has been gone all night. I was left stranded out on the road."

"You best get a posse together and go get her, sheriff."

"Aw, Judge, you know she's way out of my jurisdiction by now. That was kind of a trumped up deal anyway."

"Sheriff, you should know a posse may continue to chase a fugitive beyond their jurisdiction as long as they remain in active pursuit."

"We ain't in pursuit at all, active or otherwise."

The judge grabbed him by the elbow and steered him to the side. "You best give this some thought, Treadwell. Elections are approaching. If the word gets out that a mere trifle of a boy and an even younger girl made fools of us, we can kiss our offices goodbye."

"Oh, I see what you mean."

"We must run them to the ground, Sheriff. Justice must be served."

"We?"

"Yes, I think some daring posse service would look quite good on my record."

Treadwell smirked. "I'm sure it will, particularly against such dangerous desperados."

17

The professor headed east, going back to call on his Cherokee friends. Bryan and Carol Sue chose to go southwest, avoiding some small mountains south of them. Bryan had gotten the lay of the land in all directions from townspeople and had the old army map of the area that had the professor's route marked on it.

Almost exhausted, they finally decided to night camp in a grove of trees on a small creek. Night camp was probably not the correct term as the sky was beginning to turn a faint gray, heralding the impending sunrise. They didn't make a fire, but merely unsaddled the horses and hobbled them, then fell into their blankets and went immediately to sleep.

They slept about four hours before the sun got high enough for it's rays to make sleeping impossible. Bryan woke first and threw the blanket off, sitting up and holding his head in his hands, trying to clear the cobwebs from his mind. The movement brought Carol Sue around as well, and she sat up groggily.

"Do you know where we are?"

"More or less," he said. "I'll have to get that army map out and see what landmarks I can spot to find out for sure. Riding in the dark, it's pretty hard to keep your bearings or tell how much distance you're covering."

"I think both of us slept in the saddle some too. The horses may have changed direction some while we did."

"That's true. I hadn't thought about that."

"Which direction would they be most likely to go if they did?"

The cobwebs cleared. Bryan jumped up. "Back to the barn. Oh my goodness, do you suppose they turned around during the night. Have we been riding right back toward the people we're trying to get away from?"

He scurried over and dug the map out of his saddlebags. Grabbing his binoculars he scrambled up on a small knoll to try and get his bearings. He'd look at an area, pick out some distinguishable features of the land and try to find something like them on the map. He did this for quite some time, occasionally making some marks with a stub of a pencil.

Carol Sue built a small fire and set about preparing something to eat. She had it ready by the time she saw him coming down the hill.

"How bad is it?" she asked. "Are we in trouble?"

"No, apparently the horses stayed on course. I guess they've been out on the trail long enough that they don't think in terms of barns and corrals. It took a lot of figuring to make the landmarks match up to get a fix on where we are."

He spread the map and waited for her to get beside him where she could see. "But we're right about here. You see, here is that ridgeline, and here's the creek. The land slopes off down that way, and that line of trees way off in the distance should be the banks of the Red River."

He handed her the binoculars. "Here, you can see them with these. It's the border of the Indian Territory. Texas is on the other side."

"Texas? Oh my, I've always wanted to go there. There's something about it. Even the name has a magical sound to it."

Bryan smiled as she handed him a plate. "Yeah, I kinda feel that way myself. I've heard about Texas all my life."

"Me too."

He folded the map. "From what I've been told we shouldn't noon on this side, because this river can change in no time at all. It can rain as far away as the Rocky Mountains and the next thing you know instead of this calm lazy river, the silly thing is running deep and swift. Best to cross while we can and if it comes up then, we're already safely on the other side."

"So we should go ahead then?"

"I think so."

"We'll carry the food with us and eat it on the other side."

The professor had driven much of the night to put distance between him and Turkey Creek. He had finally watered the horses and set them out to feed and rest. He laid down in the shade of the wagon to do the same. He was awakened some time later by someone prodding him in the side with a rifle barrel.

"Come out of there, Professor."

The professor peered out from under his hat. "Ah, Sheriff, did I forget to leave your medicine?"

"This ain't about no medicine. Where are them kids?"

"Carol Sue is at the orphanage where that curmudgeon of a judge sent her."

He looked past Treadwell to the judge, who glared at him. "Bryan got mad over the whole thing and struck out on his own."

"Wrong on both counts, and you know it."

The professor crawled out from under the wagon. "I know no such thing."

Treadwell looked down at him, "The boy has absconded with the girl, and we figure you're hiding them or know where they are."

"Is that it, Sheriff, or are you here because you can track a wagon, but can't track two young people on horses?"

"Don't give me none of your lip. Where are they?"

"I have absolutely no idea."

Treadwell stepped down and snapped manacles on the professor's wrists. "Looks to me like we're gonna have to send you out to the work farm until you decide to remember. I expect it won't take much of that to help your memory. Now you get up on that wagon seat, and the boys will lead that team back to town."

"Now see here," Judge O'Dell interrupted. "We don't have time for—"

"Don't get yourself in an uproar, Judge. I'm gonna send him back with a couple of the boys. We'll send some others out to cut sign. Whoever picks up their trail can fire three shots and we'll be hot on their back trail in no time."

The Red River was reddish brown in color, a quarter of a mile wide, but not deep, and there was no problem crossing. They picked out a shady area after crossing and built a small fire to dry their clothes and prepare a meal.

Sitting by the fire Bryan said, "The way I see it we can go east, west, or south from here. East might narrow the distance between us and the sheriff, so I figure that limits the choices to two."

"Why don't you flip a coin?"

"I could do that, or we could compromise and continue to go southwest. Actually, the two closest towns going this way would be Fort Elliott, which is west of here according to this map, or Clarendon, which is more to the southwest. Clarendon is quite a bit closer, and we can follow this creek where it comes into the river to find it."

"That sounds like the best idea then, why don't we—"

"Hello there," a voice said behind them.

Carol Sue jumped and squealed. Bryan spun and reached for his pistol, but froze when he saw the star on the stranger's vest.

"I'm sorry." The man tipped his hat to Carol Sue. "Didn't mean to startle you, ma'am. I shouldn't have walked up on you that way, but I guess I figured you'd hear me coming. What are you young people doing way out here by yourselves?"

"That's a long story," Bryan said.

"I got time. I'm Clay Davidson. I'm a Texas Ranger. How about if we start with who you are?" The ranger was a big man with a full, flowing mustache. The collar length brown hair on top of skin tanned to leather by the sun made him look uncommonly tough, yet his manner was casual and his words soft and friendly.

Bryan did the introductions, and they poured the ranger some coffee. Then they related the whole story to him.

When they finished, Carol Sue looked at him with guileless eyes and said, "Are you going to take us back?"

The ranger laughed a deep, belly laugh and replied, "Young lady, there will be icicles hanging in the halls of Hades before I arrest some young dumpling like you for something like that. Near as I can see you've been cleared of the only thing that might be a crime, and now you're just being chased out of meanness. We don't hold with that sort of thing in Texas."

"So you aren't going to hold us?" Bryan asked.

"Nope."

"I'm glad to hear that because I bet that dust there is the posse. If you could help us throw our gear on the horses, we've gotta make some tracks."

"I been watching it," the ranger said. "No sense in you continuing to run. I'll talk to them."

"That won't do no good," Carol Sue's voice sounded weak.

"We'll see. This is mighty tasty coffee, miss."

The ranger sat there casually as they began to hurriedly pack their gear, but before they could finish, the posse rode up and began to cross the river.

"I make it nine," the ranger said.

"That's what I count," Bryan said.

Davidson stood up and walked over to the bank. "That'll be far enough," he shouted.

The posse pulled up in the middle of the river. "And who might you be?" Sheriff Treadwell said.

"Texas Ranger Clay Davidson. And you?"

"I'm Sheriff Jack Treadwell, and we're after those two young people you have in your possession."

"They aren't in my possession; I'm just drinking coffee with them."

Treadwell started riding closer. The ranger put his hand on his gun. "Maybe you didn't hear me, Sheriff. I said that's close enough."

Treadwell pulled up. "I'm sure they didn't tell you, Ranger, but they're fugitives."

"They told me the whole story, and my personal opinion is that you're a pack of fools chasing a couple of young people just because of their age. Out here age don't mean nuthin. We gauge people by how they stand up to trouble when it comes."

"Fools, why you . . ." Treadwell started to reach for his gun, but froze when he found himself looking into the barrels of a pair of Walker Colts.

"I think you better calm down, Sheriff, before you people get hurt. I'll save you some time. You have no jurisdiction over here. Matter of fact, you have no jurisdiction outside of your own county, but I won't get into that. You sure as blazes can't cross that river into my territory and throw your weight around. I suggest you people go home before you go and make me mad."

"There's just one of you. There's nine of us."

"Didn't I tell you I was a Texas Ranger?" he said as if that was all the explanation that was required.

Then he added, "Besides, I've got twelve friends sitting inside the chambers of these Colts, so I've got some extras if I might miss a shot or two, which I almost never do."

"And then there's us." Treadwell noticed for the first time that Bryan and Carol Sue had moved up behind him. Carol Sue had the Winchester, and Bryan had his pistol in his hand. Neither was wavering the slightest bit.

"Well, now," Davidson said, "isn't that interesting. Any of you men ever pulled a gun when somebody was ready to shoot at you? Any of you ever killed a man? Not to mention what kind of snake it would take to draw on a woman. Ain't you boys served as porch dogs for that judge long enough? Ain't it time you did your own thinking?"

"This ain't set right with me from the beginning," a cowboy behind Treadwell said.

"Me too," said another, "and I'm sure not tangling with a Texas Ranger over it."

They started turning around and riding back, leaving Treadwell and the judge sitting in the middle of the river.

"I've got half a mind to let you and this young cowboy settle it between yourselves, Sheriff. Only he'd just kill you, and I'd have to drag him back for trial. I'd get him off, of course, but it'd be an infernal nuisance."

"All right, I'm going," Treadwell said, "but if you ever get back in my jurisdiction—"

"I figure Bryan to be smarter than that," the ranger said, "but let me tell you this. I ever hear of you taking after him outside of your county again, then I'm gonna figure you don't believe in such things as a jurisdiction, and I'm gonna come boiling out of my territory to come get you. You read me, Sheriff?"

"I read you. It's not gonna be a problem. I'm over my mad. I just didn't like being called down, not even by a ranger. But to tell you the truth I didn't much like this from the beginning either. Good luck to you young folks. Just don't come back to Turkey Creek where I'd be forced to do something."

Treadwell reined around and returned to the men waiting on the other bank.

"That made me thirsty," Davidson said. "Any more of that coffee left?"

18

Seated back around the fire they continued to get acquainted. Davidson said, "You kids been traveling together all this time? . . . I mean . . . well, you know what I mean. All by yourselves?"

Carol Sue blushed and Bryan responded with an embarrassed smile. "No sir, we know that doesn't look right, and we're very much wanting to get where we can be—" He looked at Carol Sue, "What was that word?"

"Chaperoned."

"That's it. We don't want people getting the wrong idea."

"Well, I ain't been called on to do any of that, but I reckon I can ride to the next town with you. For appearance sake, of course."

"Thank you, sir."

"So what do you intend to do now?"

"Well," Bryan said, "it seems we're about to go into business with a man. "We just have to go meet up with him."

"Business, you say?"

"Yes, sir."

"At your age? Ain't that a caution? Well, I meant what I said, out here age ain't as important as getting it done, and it looks like you've got it all staked out to do." The ranger nodded in a westerly direction, "This here place you're headed for is a little town that was established by a bunch of Methodist preachers. Cowboys up this way call it Saint's Roost because it ain't got no saloons or nuthin. It's called Clarendon."

"Sounds like a nice place."

"Depends on how you look at it. I like me a little pull on the jug ever now and then, and I find it, uh, a bit confining. But there's real good folks there, and they can help you chart your course." Davidson said.

"This trail leads to it?"

"Well, like I said, I'll ride over that way with you and see how things shape up. I kinda feel like I've got an investment in this project."

Clarendon was built on the banks of Carroll creek. It was a small town with a few shops and a courthouse. Most western towns were built around the ever-present saloon. Having been founded by a group of ministers, Clarendon was built around a combination church and school building. The trio rode up to this building and found the pastor outside.

"Reverend, I've brought you a couple young people who have had them a speck of trouble. They've both lost all their kin on the trail, and they're trying to catch hold of life again."

"I see." Reverend Graham peered over his glasses at the couple. "And how old might you be?"

"I'm Bryan Wheeler, and I'm seventeen. This is Carol Sue, and she's nearly sixteen."

"That's rather young to be having such trouble."

"Yes, sir."

They went inside to talk. The building was still set up as a school and wouldn't be turned into a church until after class on Friday. They took a seat. "This sure feels funny," Bryan said.

The preacher cocked his head, "Funny?"

"It hasn't been that long since I was sitting in a classroom like this for real, but the way things have been happening it seems a lifetime ago."

The preacher smiled, "I imagine that is very true. Now suppose you tell me the whole story."

They told it again, ending with the fact that their future seemed to be with the professor and the business venture, so it was necessary to go meet him.

"You see," Bryan said, "Carol Sue and the professor are all each other has. And I don't even have that much, lessen I'm with them."

"I see," Reverend Graham nodded thoughtfully, "you need to meet back up with this man. I take it your plan is to leave her here while you go to meet this professor fellow?"

"That might be best."

Carol Sue looked shocked, "Oh no, I couldn't stand that. I couldn't let him go off and leave me."

The preacher looked at her for a long time, a gentle smile on his face. "We certainly won't try to force you as that other town did, but two young unmarried people traveling together—"

"We know that ain't seemly, preacher," Bryan said, "And we've had somebody with us the whole time except for the ride from Turkey Creek to the river."

"But what you propose is not a short ride."

"No, sir."

"Your attitude is commendable, commendable indeed, but it is poor judgment to depend on it. A smart person doesn't depend on their ability to resist temptation but instead wherever possible does not put themselves in a position where they will be tempted or go somewhere such temptation exists."

"Hasn't been no temptation," Bryan said, "we don't see each other that way. We're more like brother and sister. But I reckon there ain't no point in taking any chances. We're mighty concerned about how things look too."

"You have a point there," the preacher said. "Can you take care of her?"

Bryan told about the money he was carrying and his connection with the professor. "I figure I got enough money now to get it done. Money ain't the problem."

"A great deal of people these days are not that sure of their financial future. Well, I'm bound to ask the big question. Are your names written in the Lamb's Book of Life?"

Bryan nodded. "Preacher, I gave my heart to the Lord when I was twelve. Before we climbed in that wagon and headed west, I was at the church every time the doors were open."

"I'm so glad to hear it. And you, young lady?"

"My mother read the Bible to me a lot when I was younger and took me to church," Carol Sue said.

"And?"

"And what?"

"Have you been saved?"

She looked puzzled, "I don't know."

"That means you haven't. If you've been saved, you know it. Bryan's ticket to heaven is bought and paid for. Don't you want to be sure as well?"

"You don't think I'm going?" She became even more upset. "I've been a good person all my life."

"I'm sure you have," the preacher patted her on the arm, "but there's just one way to get to heaven. You can't get there on your own no matter how good you live."

"Bryan?" she turned to look at him.

"Yes, Carol Sue, he's telling you the straight of it. You can only get there by trusting Jesus. Have you heard of him?"

"Everybody has heard about Jesus."

Reverend Graham said, "No, actually they haven't, but we won't go into that. You know the story of Jesus?"

"Yes, about Him being crucified and coming back out of the grave?"

"Precisely. You know why He was crucified?"

She shook her head, "Not really."

"He was crucified to pay for our sins. God hates sin and Jesus willingly gave Himself as a sacrifice for us. Do you believe that?"

"Yes, I've heard that, and I do believe it."

"Then all you have to do is tell Jesus you believe in Him and ask Him to save you. He's ready to do it."

"That's all there is to it?"

"It isn't hard. But He knows if you mean it or not when you pray the prayer."

They knelt together and the preacher helped her pray the sinner's prayer. When they finished, the three stood there with their hands joined. They looked over at Davidson, who had been quietly standing off to the side.

"Ranger, do you mind if I ask—"

"Save your breath, Parson, I've done too many things that wouldn't square with the Good Book. I've dispatched a number of people to heaven or hell, I don't know which. I reckon my course is charted, and there ain't much I can do about it."

"I'm sorry to hear that. A lot of people look up to you. Your example could do a lot of good."

"Maybe we can talk about it some time, Preacher, but I'm not in the mood for it right now."

Graham shook his head as he watched the big ranger walk away, then he turned and smiled at the young couple. "I think I have a good idea of your situation now, and I may have a solution for you."

"What's that?"

"If you are bound and determined to go on, but want to do the right thing, you need another chaperone."

Bryan nodded, "We know that."

"There is a man by the name of Scott Mackey has a little hardscrabble farm south of town. He and his wife Janet have had a tough time of it. He's looking for work."

"That's pretty tough," Bryan frowned, "are you saying we should get us a hired hand?"

"I am. You appear to have the resources for it, and it would solve your chaperone problem as well as help them out of a bind."

"But a grown man working for a kid my age?"

"I believe you would find him very amenable to it, and you need to get past thinking of yourself as a kid. Maybe you didn't feel you were ready to do it, but you've been carrying a man's load from what I can tell, and that doesn't appear it will change anytime soon."

19

Scott and Janet Mackey were in the lobby of the hotel when Bryan came down the next morning, "The reverend told us you were looking for a hired man," he said.

"Yes, sir. You sure you wouldn't have a problem working for somebody my age?"

"I have a lot of respect for anybody who has managed to be financially secure at such a young age. As you can see, I'm not doing that well."

Bryan smiled. "Maybe we can help you change that, help each other in the process."

"Does that mean I'm hired?"

"It does."

Janet spoke up, "We were told there is a young lady."

"Yes, I knocked on her door as I came down. Reckon she'll be down any—"

They looked up at the same time to see Carol Sue coming down the stairs. Janet said, "Why, she's lovely."

"She sure is," Bryan agreed.

The work farm was a collection of shacks, pure and simple. The professor was transported to it shackled in the back of a wagon. He was dumped in front of one of them, then roughly pushed inside. It took a minute for his eyes to adjust to the darkness. It was rows of bunks, and the stench was overpowering.

"Bunk down at the end is open," the burly guard said. "Owner died this morning."

"Lucky him," somebody nearby said.

The guard took the chains off and he went in search of the bunk. *I'm too soft for this,* he thought. *I don't think I can do it.* He smiled. *But I know my limitations, that's why I insisted they not tell me their plans. I can't tell what I don't know.*

He collapsed on the bunk, indescribably tired. *I wonder how long it'll take to get used to this smell.*

"It don't take long."

"Excuse me?"

"The smell, it don't take long to get used to it."

He turned on his side. The speaker was a wiry little man with most of his teeth missing. "How could you possibly know I was thinking that?"

"It's the first thing everybody thinks." He looked the professor over. "Whatcha in for? Debtor?"

"No, I'm in for protecting a young lady's freedom."

"That so? Never heard of that one before."

While the ladies got packed to go, Bryan and Scott got them outfitted for the trail. They traded off the packhorse and the sorrel Carol Sue had been riding and purchased a ranch wagon. Covered, but smaller than the big Conestoga wagons favored on the wagon trains, it was a comfortable ride with its spring-mounted driver's seat. It carried all of their belongings easily and still provided room to bed down out of the elements. Bryan kept his horse Patches, and Scott would ride his own saddle horse.

They got a fresh set of provisions packed and ready to go. The reverend and Judge White saw them off and extracted a promise that they would return. "If you're going to go into business, there's no better place to do it than Clarendon," the judge said.

As the little wagon trailed down the road headed back to the southeast, Carol Sue was mounted riding with Bryan as an outrider while Scott drove. They turned and waved to those standing out wishing them farewell. Three young boys on ponies raced around them like yapping dogs before finally returning to town.

Bryan rode next to Carol Sue. She looked at him and said, "I still can't believe how they took us in. How much they did for us."

"Friendliest place I've ever been."

"Will we come back like you said?"

"I think we'll have to talk to the professor before we can know that."

She sighed. Finally she raised her head and said, "You know, I haven't even asked where we're going."

Bryan laughed, "I wondered when you were going to get around to asking."

"To tell the truth, I've been so caught up in all this that I just plain didn't care, but it's time."

He laughed again, "All right, reach into my saddlebags and get that army map."

She got it and opened it out. "You see that pencil line connecting the towns?"

"Yes, I saw that when you were showing me where we were before."

"That's the route the professor marked where he'd be going. You see it goes east out of Turkey Creek over into the Cherokee country? Then it turns down and goes into east Texas through various towns, then back towards Ft. Worth."

"Yes, I see. The line stops there?"

"He figured we'd have caught up with him by then, or I was to send a wire to Ft. Worth, and he'd come running."

"I see. So we just keep going backwards around this circle until we meet him?"

"That sounds like the best bet to me."

"It sounds like a pleasant little journey."

It was indeed a pleasant trip for several days. They felt they had to be getting close to Ft. Worth. Bryan and Carol Sue were again riding behind the wagon as she was talking about how much the country had changed. "There's so much to see. Look at those men over there, for example. Aren't they magnificent?"

"What men?" Bryan looked around to see several Indians sitting ponies atop a small rise.

"Look at the beautiful colors, the feathers and bright colored shields. And that bright colored paint on their faces."

Scott had already whipped the team into a run as he turned them toward some nearby rocks "Would you quit gawking at them and get going. That pretty paint is war paint. Those are Comanche, and it looks like a raiding party."

"You mean they're unfriendly?"

Bryan pulled his pistol as he looked back. "These aren't boys this time. This is the real thing." He was puzzled. The warriors had not moved.

Why aren't they chasing us?

Then he knew. Scott discovered it at the same time and sawed hard on the left reins, turning from the rocks sweeping down toward a small gully further away. Shots rang out from the boulders where they were headed, and they heard the nasty whine of bullets passing close.

"Are they shooting at us?"

"Those aren't bees buzzing around our head."

Bryan turned into the gully sending wet sand showering. He raced down the bank to pull up in a little horseshoe where the creek turned. "Get down and get behind the wagon." He jumped down and pulled the pin on the doubletree, leading the team behind the wagon. Then he pulled his saddle horse back there as well.

"This isn't a very big wagon for all of us to try and hide behind," he said.

He looked up. "We were lucky to find this overhang, though. That'll keep them from getting behind us, and they can't shoot down on us."

They could hear scuffling sounds above them and falling dirt hit the outside edge of the wagon cover. "Guess they just found that out." Scott grinned a nervous grin.

Bryan took the Winchester and levered a shell into it. He offered Carol Sue his pistol. "Can you shoot this?"

She nodded, trembling violently.

"Easy now, we've got us a good position here. Don't be counting us out yet. This is real easy to use. You see this little notch in the back? You sight down through it with your arm out straight. You look at this little knob on the end of the gun and you put it in front of somebody you don't like. Then you take a deep breath, hold it and squeeze the trigger slowly, don't jerk it."

"Holding my breath won't be a problem. I haven't breathed in ten minutes."

"A quick prayer wouldn't hurt anything, to test your new-found relationship with the Creator."

"I've been working on that too."

"I just can't figure out why they haven't been chasing us. At first it was because we were running right into their little trap, but when we ducked out of it . . . well, I just don't know."

"Maybe they just aren't in a hurry."

"You're probably right. They figure us to be easy and just want to look us over first."

In a few minutes, a line of Indians approached across the river and pulled up. "I make it twenty or so," Scott said.

"Yes, I was just counting them," Bryan agreed. "It's too many, isn't it?"

Actually, one Comanche warrior is probably too many, green as I am, but I can't let her know that.

"No, we've got good cover, and they're going to have to cross the creek to get at us. We'll be all right. Just don't waste bullets. Don't pull that trigger until you're sure it's lined up on one of them."

The Comanche were talking among themselves in an agitated manner. Their voices were getting louder and louder.

Suddenly three of them put heels to their horses and came forward, yelping and leaning low over the necks of the horses.

"Wait now, just wait."

The warriors came fast, but instead of crossing the water they turned parallel to the wagon and swung down behind the bodies of their horses. They fired under the horse's necks, bullets hitting the wagon and the bluff behind. Those behind the wagon held their fire.

The warriors finished their pass and turned back. The third Indian sat up too soon. Bryan had been tracking them with his rifle, so he pulled the trigger and the man slumped forward.

"Now they know we can hit what we're aiming at," he said.

"You shot him?"

"He was trying to shoot us."

"I never saw a man shot. I don't think I can—"

"I didn't want to do it, but we have no choice. You'll do what you have to do when the time comes."

The warriors were still talking in an animated fashion. Two braves had gotten down and seemed to be tending to the one on the ground.

"I don't think I killed him. He seems to have made it back to his friends."

"Now what?"

"I figure that was only a probing attack," Scott said, "to see what we're made of. They'll probably come in force now. When they hit that water, you shoot as fast as you can, but try to line up a target. You have six bullets, so don't waste them and count your shots."

An overpowering din of screeches and yelps erupted and the Comanche rushed them in a line. Bryan started lining up his shots and one pitched forward as he pulled the trigger. They came across the creek this time and both began firing as fast as they could. The noise was deafening. Trying to come up the slope in the soft sand slowed the horses and gave the travelers time to shoot and three more warriors fell. They were scooped up and the charge broke.

"We ran them off." Carol Sue said, "I can't believe it."

"Get the guns loaded quick," Bryan said. "They'll be back."

Carol Sue started reloading furiously.

"Oh no,"

They turned at the sound of Janet's voice. Scott lay face down behind them, an arrow sticking out of his back.

Bryan jumped to his side. "He's breathing; he's alive."

Janet worked to make Scott comfortable as Bryan thumbed shells into his Winchester. He was counting heads. "There's still better than a dozen mounted, but that's plenty. Get ready, they're about to come again, and this time I doubt if we can stop them."

With yells like marauding wolves the Commanches started forward again, low on their horses. Before they reached the stream a rider came up to intercept them. They pulled up sharply just out of rifle range.

Carol Sue didn't understand. "What's going on?"

"I don't know. We were lucky with that first rush; they'll probably ride over us this time." He watched the rider come up and begin talking excitedly, pointing toward them. "Wait a minute, that's the young Comanche I had the tussle with. I told you about him."

"What's he doing?"

"You got me. He don't speak English."

They finished speaking and sat there looking toward the wagon for several moments. Then the large warrior with all the feathers rode forward. He stopped outside of camp and said, "Where is the young white man that fought with my son?"

Bryan stood up.

"Pony That Walks says you fought him with honor and could have taken his life, but you did not."

"It wasn't necessary."

"You did this even after an attack on your people?"

Bryan nodded.

"I thought you to be weak for not taking his life after you had bested him. But not doing so after that attack would take great strength. You gave him his life. I give your life to you."

He looked toward the wagon and the people huddled behind it. "You helped my daughter too."

"Your daughter?"

The war chief looked at him as if he was a puzzle to him, "She is called Morning Star. You helped her at great risk to yourself. I do not understand why you did so."

"It was the right thing to do."

"I am greatly in your debt. I give you not only your life, but the lives of those who are with you."

The big warrior threw his war lance in the dirt leaving it sticking up like a marker. Still with no sign of emotion on his face he said, "Go in peace. If you should ever find yourself in the land of the Comanche, keep this lance and show it as your blue-bellies show their flag. You will be under my protection."

20

Bryan walked back to the wagon. Scott said, "What just happened?"

Bryan shook his head, "Near as I can tell I didn't kill his son when I could have, and the girl I rescued from Fat Jack turned out to be his daughter."

"Are you kidding?"

"Do I look like I'm kidding?" Bryan held up the lance. "Not only that, it seems this war lance guarantees our protection from any Comanche we might see."

Scott was impressed. "All that just because you helped a couple of people even though they were different from you."

"It looks that way."

They made camp right where they were. Just as they got a fire going to heat water and tend to Scott's wound they heard Davidson yell, "Hello the camp."

"Hello yourself, come on in," Bryan responded.

The ranger rode in and tied off his horse. He pushed his hat back on his head. "Are you two all right? There's some mighty interesting tracks out there. It looks to me like you've had yourselves quite a party."

"That's for sure."

"I have to admit I'm surprised you were able to stand 'em off."

"I think the Lord stepped in. I can't make it add up any other way."

The ranger came around the wagon to see Scott lying there. He moved to him quickly. "We have to get this arrow out of him and get him to a doctor."

Bryan nodded, "I was about to try and do that. I sure am glad to see you. None of us have done anything like that before."

"We need some cloths, some of that hot water, and hold this in the fire until it gets really hot." Davidson handed his knife to Bryan and walked over to his horse. He pulled a bottle of whiskey out of his saddlebag.

Carol Sue frowned at him, "Do you have to do that now?"

The ranger grinned, "It's for my hands, and that knife."

He poured it over his hands and rubbed them together, then knelt by Scott. "Find a little stick and put it between his teeth. Don't want him breaking anything if he clamps down." He looked down at the injured man. "You ready for this. It's going to hurt, but I'll try to make it quick. You want a pull on this bottle?"

"I don't drink."

"This ain't about drinking, pardner, this is the only painkiller I got to help you."

He nodded and took a big swig of the alcohol. "Yuk," he said. "You drink this stuff on purpose?"

"You get used to it. Hit it again, big slug."

"How bad is it?" Janet's face was a mask of concern.

"I ain't no doctor, but I seen lots of wounds, and this looks like it's just in the fleshy part of the shoulder. One more time on that jug, friend."

Scott grinned. "It doesn't taste as bad as it did."

The ranger looked at Janet. "One thing about somebody that don't drink hitting it for the first time, it don't take much to get the job done."

"He isn't going to become a drunk now is he?"

Davidson laughed, "Takes more than trying it one time to get hooked on it. Unless he just really decides he likes it."

Her mouth set in a firm line. "I think I can help him make that decision."

"I'll just bet you can. Bryan, you get a firm grip on that right arm and shoulder and hold him steady. You ladies catch hold too. I don't want him moving."

Davidson made a quick cut to give room to pull the arrowhead out, bathed the area with the alcohol, and used a needle and thread provided by the ladies to close the cut. "I think he's going to do fine. It don't look like it hit anything vital."

He put a bandage on it then helped Scott sit up. "You showed a lot of guts friend; you hardly made a sound."

"Hard to yell and clamp down on a stick at the same time."

"That so?" Davidson grinned. "I've been able to get 'er done a couple of times."

Davidson made a sling for his arm, then tied it with another cloth around his torso so it'd be secure up against his body. "That'll hold you until we get on in to town."

They bedded Scott down in the wagon. He fell asleep immediately. Davidson said, "Best thing for him right now. Let's let him sleep a bit, then we'll head on to town."

He looked over at Carol Sue. "You guys are either the luckiest folks I ever seen or you got some mighty powerful help."

"You talking about God?" Bryan said. "I thought you told that preacher you didn't believe in God."

"No, I didn't say that. I said I'm just too far down the trail to do anything about it."

"I don't believe that."

"Somehow I didn't figure you would. Listen, let's save that for later, I want to hear more about how you got that war party to go away." The ranger was drinking his coffee outright, seemingly oblivious to the fresh-from-the-fire temperature. "Gotta say you handled yourself good though. From the tracks I'd say you accounted for yourself pretty good before you got that help. I'd say you're a good shot."

"I've kept meat on the table since I was a button. At least I'm pretty fair with the rifle. I'm no great shakes with a hand gun."

"A gun's a tool, like anything else. Gotta learn how to use them right and practice."

"Will you show me?

"Sure. Let me see it first, holster and all."

The ranger drained his cup and set it beside him, extending a hand toward Bryan.

He must have a rock-lined throat. Bryan unbuckled his belt and handed it over.

Davidson worked the gun in and out of the holster several times, holding it in his lap. It wouldn't have even come close to buckling on him.

"Okay, this is a fair rig, but it kinda binds."

"I traded the professor for it," Bryan said. "The gun belt Fat Jack wore would have looped around me three times."

Davidson chuckled, "Let's see what we can do about it." He pulled out a razor sharp knife and cut a V in the front of the holster.

"There. That keeps the hammer of the gun from dragging. Now, while I work on this pistol a bit, why don't you rub the inside of this holster with a little of your gun oil. It's a good idea to rub it down good every time you clean your guns. Will generally be enough oil left on the rag you use in the cleaning to get the job done. Don't leave a film on it; that'll drag. Just work a little into the leather. It'll keep it soft too."

"What are you doing?"

"Gonna take this file I use to trim my horse's hooves and use it to remove this front sight."

"Wait a minute, I won't be able to aim!"

"Sure you will. You don't aim a pistol like a rifle. Don't have a big long barrel to line up. You just learn to point a pistol like you point your finger. It's for close work. Pull and point, pull and point; practice until it comes natural."

Davidson finished working with the file. "There, that comes out right smooth now. You buckle it back on."

Bryan cinched it down tight.

"All right, son, now speed ain't everything here. Many a man has beat another guy to the draw only to spray bullets all over the room while his target is calmly going ahead and shooting him. So taking the time to get on line is the main thing, but the quicker a guy can do that and do it right, the better. First off, you've wearing that holster too low. It oughta hang where it puts the gun butt up above your wrist."

"Like this?" Bryan frowned. "That don't seem right. Looks like it ought to be where your hand is right there so you don't have to pull it far before it clears."

"Trust me and give it a try. Now let your hand hang so your fingers are along the side of the holster, but where your thumb very lightly touches the front of it. Good. Now very slowly, move your hand up to where the thumb makes contact with the hammer on the gun and stop."

Bryan did as he was told. Davidson repositioned it slightly. "You want this part of your thumb here to make the contact, just above the ball of the joint. That gives you a secure pull. Practice making that contact several times until it starts to feel natural. Pick up on the gun a little each time, then stop. I'm gonna get me some more coffee."

He returned and watched for a bit. "That looks good." At the top of the next motion he said, "Now freeze. Look at your hand. When the thumb starts to lift that gun, look at where your fingers are. You just tuck them around that handle and continue pulling the gun, but stop as you start to clear leather. You practice the motion up to there, over and over while I drink this coffee."

Bryan practiced while the ranger finished, then had another cup. Finally he said, "Good, that's real smooth. You have a natural talent for this. Now comes the most important part of all. As that barrel clears, you pop it on line with your target. It's a snapping motion, like this, elbow tucked in tight. And as that finger slides into the trigger guard you point the finger at the target. It'll point the gun. If you're a believing man you may not have much experience pointing fingers at folks, but for most of us it comes real natural."

Bryan tried the motion.

"Fine, real fine. You have three motions now, and you have to put them together into one quick snap, but a move that ends with your elbow locked and the gun on line. You just keep practicing until it feels natural to you."

"Shouldn't I be shooting as I do it?"

"One thing at a time. You see why this is faster yet?"

"It feels good, but it still doesn't seem logical."

"People who wear the gun level with their hand have to grab the gun butt and pull the pistol with it. They have to use their thumb to cock the weapon as they are pulling it. This way, the thumb makes the first contact and the momentum of your hand as it's already moving makes the whole thing work in one smooth motion."

"Pretty slick."

Carol Sue said, "When you boys are through playing you might come get this food, before I have to throw it out."

Davidson smiled. "Now why do you suppose it is that everybody in the world that cooks threatens to throw out the food?"

Bryan returned the smile. "I've heard it all my life."

"You'd think after they worked that hard on it, that tossing it would be the furtherest thing from their mind."

"You would think that, wouldn't you?"

"You guys are just *too* funny. Get yourself a plate and I'll dish you up some stew."

"Hey Judge, guess what I found?"

"Some dignity, perhaps?" Judge O'Dell looked at Treadwell standing in the door of his office.

The lawman didn't get the intended slight.

"I see that isn't it, so what then?"

"This here is the professor's account book." He walked over to show the small journal to the judge. "He's got notations of deals in it, things he's bought and where he's found the ingredients to make his snake oil."

"Fascinating." The judge slipped his glasses on and looked at it. "I suppose you are thinking of giving up your badge and taking over his trade?"

"Not likely, but I did get to noticing all the entries are always made in the same order."

"I underestimated you, Sheriff. You've discovered the man follows a route?"

"He sure does." Treadwell looked pleased with himself.

"How interesting," he handed the book back and rocked back in his chair, "so even if they didn't tell him their plans, chances are they know the route and are planning to meet up with him somewhere on it."

"You think so?"

The judge shook his head. "I wouldn't have said it if I didn't."

"What good does it do us to know that?"

The judge made an openhanded gesture. "All we have to do is follow the route and we'll have them."

Treadwell's eyes widened, and he took an involuntary step backwards, "Oh no, not me, that ranger done told me what was going to happen if he caught me doing that."

"Sheriff, elections are almost here, and we're the butt of every joke told in town after what they did to us. We have to set this right."

"I told you the ranger said—"

"That ranger is long gone," the judge said icily. "Texas is a very big state."

"It ain't big enough for me and him both."

"Treadwell, you have no choice. Without that badge you can't survive. You're too lazy to work and too dumb to steal."

The sheriff frowned. "Now I don't have to put up with . . ."

"Think now," the judge talked slowly as if speaking to a young child. "Don't get your back up in the air. You know I'm right, even if it does offend your delicate sensibilities."

"Well, I have to admit it's really all I know how to do."

"That's more like it. Get a map, and let's do a little figuring."

Riding on to Ft. Worth the next day the practice sessions continued. Davidson had Bryan start including target practice when they stopped. Bryan was indeed a natural.

"Pulling that trigger is the last part of the motion," Davidson said. "Don't jerk it, but it finishes the pull in one smooth action, snap and pull."

He started indicating targets and Bryan kept hitting closer and closer. "I never saw anybody take to it so quickly," Davidson said with a smile.

"Will I ever be as fast as you?"

"Shucks, son, I ain't fast, and you really don't want to try to get that way. I'm deadly though. I hit what I shoot at. People may be faster, but don't nobody get a second shot at me, even if they hit me with the first one. You'd be surprised how often fast guns miss that first one."

"I thought what I was trying to do—"

"What you're trying to do is learn to get that gun in play smoothly and efficiently. Trust me, you don't want no reputation with it. It'd hound you the rest of your natural life. But pulling it on a man is the last thing in the world you ever want to do. That should only be if you've tried everything in the world to keep it from happening."

"I understand," Bryan said. "Trust me, the last thing I ever want to do is shoot somebody again. I didn't even want to shoot at those Comanche when I had it to do."

"That's the right attitude." He looked toward the wagon and raised his voice. "How's our patient doing?"

Janet stuck her head out the back. "He's pretty comfortable. Every now and then a large bump gets his attention but he's doing all right."

Ft. Worth was situated on the banks of the Trinity River, built right on the edge of an army camp as the name implied. Actually, the town was so close to the camp, that the Officers Quarters made up one side of the town square. There were businesses situated at other points around the square.

They left the wagon and stock at the wagon yard to venture downtown. It had dirt streets, and the town square had a half-built courthouse in the middle of it. Davidson explained it.

"The courthouse construction started before the war when there were around six thousand people here, but nearly the whole population went off with a regiment of Confederate Calvary, the Ninth Texas. Reckon they're having trouble getting it finished."

A two-story hotel called Steele's Tavern faced the courthouse. In spite of the name, it had a parlor and a sitting room for ladies and featured a first-class dining room.

Davidson said, "This is where I have to take my leave. I got to get back to Austin. The doctor's office is upstairs above the general store."

Carol Sue turned to look up at him. "I sure hate to see you go. We owe you so very much."

"Yes, Clay, that goes double for me," Janet said. "I hate to think what might have happened without you."

The ranger removed his hat as she turned to him. "Glad I could be of help, ma'am. I've surely enjoyed your company."

Bryan extended his hand. "Can't you at least have dinner with us before you leave?"

"I got to hit the trail, but you're going to enjoy the food here. The chef came here from New Orleans, and he knows his business. It's real fancy grub. What if this professor guy ain't here?"

Bryan shook his head. "We're going to go look, but I think his wagon would have been there where we left ours."

"Whatcha plan on doing now, then?"

Bryan walked to the edge of the boardwalk. "I think we'll treat ourselves to a night or two in the hotel, then we'll start backtracking the route he marked on the map I showed you."

"That's a right fine idea. Well, if you ever need me, you just wire Ranger headquarters, they'll know how to get hold of me."

He touched his hand to his hat brim in one last salute to Carol Sue, swung his horse in one quick motion, jerked his heels, and the horse was gone in a half-dozen jackrabbit steps.

Bryan grinned. "Davidson has style and maybe a little flair for the dramatic. He'd be mighty hard for a guy to compete with."

Carol Sue nodded, "Oh, he's all man and a yard wide. Takes a girl's breath away. But the love of his life is action and danger. Any girl who has her head on straight wants a man whose life is wrapped up in her, not in what's over the next hill."

He smiled. "That may be good to know."

She added quietly. "But I wouldn't lie to you, he's mighty exciting to be around."

He threw his head back and laughed. "I got news for you, he's exciting for guys to be around as well."

21

The doctor praised Davidson's work. He put a fresh bandage on and taped it to immobilize it again. "I think you'll find as long as your shoulder won't move that the pain won't be too bad, but I'll give you some pain pills just in case."

They got settled in the hotel, and Scott went to bed, Janet sitting up beside him. Bryan and Carol Sue wanted to try the fancy dining the ranger had told them about, but Janet didn't want to come. They said they'd bring something back for her.

The restaurant was called Maxim's. It was a serious attempt at big city elegance, right in the middle of a rough and tumble cow town. The waiter who came to serve them wore evening clothes.

"My name is Hobson, sir, may I bring you something to drink?" He placed large, ornate menus in front of them. They contained a lot of entrées with names they did not recognize and contained no prices.

"May I be truthful with you, Hobson?" Bryan said.

Hobson's face appeared to be made of stone. "I live for that possibility, sir."

"You may have already figured out that we're a little young and inexperienced at this sort of thing."

He inclined his head slightly. "It had occurred to me, sir."

"I gotta tell you this menu might as well be written in Greek for all the good it does me."

"I'm not surprised. Sir, most of the names of the entrées are written in French."

"Oh, so that's it," Bryan shrugged. "That makes me feel better anyway. How are we supposed to know what we're eating?"

Hobson leaned down close. "You could do like a lot of my patrons and pretend like you understand fully, act like you are mispronouncing the names on purpose as a lark, and order me around in a loud voice. Then just take your chances on what you might actually receive to eat."

Bryan shook his head, "I don't think I'd like to do that. It's not exactly my style."

"Ah, too bad sir, I do enjoy that little game so."

His sarcasm was not lost on the couple, and Carol Sue hid a laugh behind her menu.

Bryan stayed with it, "Which brings me back to my problem."

"May I suggest two options, sir? You might peruse the menu and ask me about anything that looks interesting to you. In such a case I shall endeavor to tell you what it is, how it is prepared, and what it costs."

"I hate to put you to that much trouble."

"It is no trouble. That is what I am employed here to do and seldom get the opportunity. Besides," something that was almost a smile came over his face, although it looked more like a grimace, "when I work that hard, I usually get an obscenely large gratuity."

"What's a gratuity?"

"A tip, sir, a reward for extraordinary service."

He lowered his voice to take them into his confidence. "I might add the 'what it is' portion of that offer might be useful, as our cook is Cajun French and has a tendency to consider some things as delicacies which others often consider as inedible items."

"You said there were two options?"

"I certainly did, sir. You might simply place yourself in my hands, and I would undertake to handcraft a memorable evening for you. Patrons seldom select that option. People in this part of the world have a strong tendency to be rather stubborn about being in control of their own destiny. In fact, I seldom offer this particular service to people, but your candor in soliciting my assistance encourages me to do so."

Bryan laid his menu aside. "Putting ourselves in your hands sounds great to me."

He looked at Carol Sue, and she nodded her assent.

"That is the best selection on the menu if I might be permitted to say so. Now, may I inquire as to whether there is a set budget for this excursion?"

"Huh?"

Hobson sighed. "How much did you wish to spend?"

"Oh, that. We aren't rich, but we're pretty well-heeled, and since we're celebrating, we would like to cut loose the weasel a bit, so the sky's the limit."

"How colorful! Maxim's specializes in *cutting loose the weasel*. And may I ask the occasion for the celebration?"

"You may. It is Carol Sue's birthday."

"A very special birthday," Carol Sue said.

"Congratulations, birthday you say? That makes it an even more interesting challenge, and I shall certainly redouble my efforts to make it most memorable."

He looked at Carol Sue. "And you, miss, have you any preferences I should keep in mind in my planning?"

"I think I'd like something dainty, even frilly. Something out of the ordinary."

"Everything Chef Louie cooks is out of the ordinary. Some of it he does not even recognize himself."

He reached out for the menus. "I think I can remove these, unless you are still enjoying reading them." They surrendered them with a grin.

"Could I trouble you to follow me?"

They both looked confused. "I fear I have seated you in the wrong place. You see, we compose our seating as part of the atmosphere. We make sure those we expect to have an extraordinary dining experience in the most visible place in the center of the room. We find that encourages those around them. I apologize, but I took you for very casual diners. In the light of this new information and your obvious sophistication, I would like to humbly correct my error and move you to the center of the dais, a station much more suitable for the experience to follow."

He escorted them to a table overlooking the room. He seated Carol Sue remarking, "Entertainment will start shortly, a rather excellent pianist with a classical repertoire, and this is the very best location to enjoy it. I hope you are not in a hurry, as I think we will be spending the evening together."

"Hobson," Bryan said, "we surrender ourselves completely to your care."

"I'm delighted, sir. You won't regret it. I think we shall start with a little hors d'oeuvres accompanied by a light blush wine."

Carol Sue's face lit up. "What are those?"

"Hor d'oeuvres, ma'am? Appetizers. In this case I think a selection would be in order. The chef has some marvelous broiled shrimp with this delicate little cocktail sauce that is a standard. He has some stuffed crab that is excellent and I think perhaps a few of his seafood items prepared to be dipped in the same sauce."

Bryan looked at her. "I've never had any seafood before, have you?"

Carol Sue said, "I never imagined it would even be available this far from the gulf."

"We go to extraordinary lengths to make it available. It is iced down in a wagon that is driven from Galveston in shifts, day and night, to get it here as expeditiously as possible."

They both indicated they hadn't had it before.

"Then you are in for a wonderful treat," Hobson said.

"I've just had catfish and bass and other things I've caught."

"A similar experience, only this will be more delectable. It does lose a little in being transported in a wagon load of ice as opposed to being down on the coast and eating it fresh from the water. You really should treat yourself to that experience some day, but I think for now it shall serve our purpose admirably."

"Ah," Bryan beckoned the waiter to come close. Hobson leaned near, and he said, "I hate to put any restrictions on what you're doing, but we don't really hold with drinking alcohol, if you know what I mean."

Hobson straightened up. "Very prudent, sir, we have a delightful non-alcoholic sparkling cider, but which should compliment the meal admirably.

It was excellent. Carol Sue's dainty fare turned out to be shrimp basted in a garlic butter sauce and served on a bed of Cajun rice with steamed vegetables on the side. Bryan was served a sampler of several fish and crab entrées, with small bowls of various sauces to dip them in. The cider selection was as complimentary as he had promised. The dessert turned out to something with a name neither recognized, but which arrived at the table, fully ablaze much to their alarm.

As the evening finally ended Bryan said, "Hobson, you have outdone yourself."

"It has been a delight, sir. The entire staff has been caught up in our presentation at some point."

★　　　★　　　★

Three days later they tried to leave Scott and Janet in Ft. Worth to recuperate but they wouldn't hear of it. "We signed on for the trip, and we're going to hold up our end." Scott said. "Besides, the pain is tolerable, and I'd have it whether I was wallowing around in a bed or riding on this wagon seat."

Bryan had to relent.

Carol Sue was still floating as they pointed their wagon east. "That was wonderful!"

"Yes, it was nice."

"No, not nice, *wonderful*! You men just have to be so . . . so . . . close-mouthed. Like the world would come to an end if anybody found out you were happy or sad."

"I'm sorry."

She rode close to him. "Oh, I'm not complaining, I suppose it all has to do with being manly. But sometimes—"

"I'll work on it."

"Well, going back to what I was saying, I think—"

"Owww!"

They looked at Scott, "You having pain?"

He turned around and started fishing around in the back. "Something prodded me in the . . . well, my goodness, Davidson forgot his shotgun."

Scott pulled the short-barreled scatter gun out from behind the seat. "Imagine that."

Bryan smiled. "From what I've seen of Davidson, he'd be more likely to forget his head. My guess is he intended us to have it. Be just like him to leave it and not say anything. More of that manly stuff you were talking about. I figure he left it for you," he said to Carol Sue.

"But why would I need . . ."

"He knows you aren't familiar with guns. Don't have to be a good shot with that thing."

"What an unusual present."

"Not out here, it ain't." Scott said. "Right practical I'd say. And special too. I expect he thought a lot of that gun."

"I'd rather have had a dozen roses, but it was sweet of him in its own way. But I don't want to think about guns and bad things. All that is behind us. I want to think about those fabulous meals and all of the sights that we saw. It was just too much."

"I'm glad you enjoyed it."

"There you go again. Enjoyed it is such an understatement. I'm a small town girl. I've never done anything like that in my life. It was a wonderland. I had such fun. I wish it didn't have to end."

"Good things have to end, at least for a time."

"Why?"

"Don't you see? If we go back again, it'll be just as wonderful next time. But say we moved there and tried to make it last forever, inside of a couple of weeks we'd just be residents and we'd take it all for granted. It wouldn't be wonderful any more. People can only take so much wonderful at one time."

"You know, I think you may be right. What a marvelous insight."

"Even a blind hog finds an acorn every now and then."

"A blind hog indeed. Don't you go selling yourself short, Bryan Wheeler."

22

Bryan cleared his throat. "The name of this town we're coming to is Nacogdodoches. It was an Indian village long before any white men ever came to this country. The town was named after the Nacogdoche Indians. This here road we're on is the *El Camino Real* or the King's Highway."

Carol Sue was amazed. "Where'd you find out so much about it? Have you been here before?"

"No, I just made it my business to find out what I could about everything that's on our route. Here, let's get over to the wagon yard and see what we can find out."

At the wagon yard they asked the hostler to tend to their team, to include a good bait of grain. Then they walked down the main street to the business district. It was built around an old stone fort that was the first structure that had been built in the area.

They walked into the general store where a man perched on a ladder peered at them over his glasses and said, "Can I hep ya?"

"Do you know Professor Harold Donovan?" Bryan asked.

"Everybody knows the professor."

"We were to meet up with him. He has this on his route. Do you know if he's arrived yet?"

The man came down the ladder and turned to them, wiping his hands on his apron. "You been down at the livery?"

"We left our wagon there."

"That'd be his first stop, and he'd come here or to see the doc next. Doc's out birthing a baby, and the professor ain't been in here."

"He hasn't been at the wagon yard either, so I guess he hasn't arrived yet."

"You gonna wait on him?"

"I don't know. We are backtracking his route hoping to meet him. If he doesn't show tomorrow I think we'll continue that plan."

"Well, I hope he makes it soon; I'm running mighty low on his patent medicines. He makes really good potions, you know?"

"Yes, we know. We've invested in his business and plan on helping him make it grow and prosper."

"I'd say that was a solid investment. You got room for somebody else to buy in?"

"Can't say. We'd have to discuss that with him."

"I'd be interested."

"We'll ask."

"Long as you people are going to be around, Sammy Tucker is going to be sawing on his fiddle over at the schoolhouse tonight. He'll have a couple of good side men, maybe as much as a five-piece band. Big doings. You'd be more than welcome, particularly if you'll share these pretty ladies for a few dances."

"It ain't up to me. I have no say over these ladies. But I might get a bit testy if'n anybody didn't treat them respectful."

"The fellows will be most polite and respectful, I can assure you." The storekeeper turned his attention to the ladies, "It'd be appreciated if you share a few dances. Don't get much female companionship out this way."

"Well," Carol Sue smiled, "I for one would be in favor of attending a social, at which time I would decide for myself if and when I might choose to dance with someone."

CHAPTER 22

"Yes, ma'am. Of course."

Janet walked over. "I'm afraid I don't dance, but thank you so much for the offer."

"Hope you'll plan on coming to the social anyway. Just having your company would be mighty nice."

"My husband has recently had some health difficulties. I'll have to see how he feels when the time comes."

"Yes, ma'am. Can't ask no more than that."

"That was a nice party," Carol Sue commented as they headed out of town, waving to a few folks on the way.

"Yes, it was."

She folded her hands in her lap, "We seem to be making good friends in every town we come to."

"If you don't count the reception we got in Turkey Creek, I'd say that was true. We're right lucky, but part of that is you. You want to be friends with everybody, and they respond to that. I'm a lucky guy to be teamed up with a girl like you."

She grabbed onto his arm. "I figure I'm the lucky one."

"I guess we're just both lucky."

They were following an old Indian trace. It wasn't as good a trail, but it would get them to the same place. They didn't feel very comfortable going by the river trail.

23

They were a half day out of Shreveport. The trace had turned onto a well-traveled trail. The land had flattened out, but still had a lot of greenery and vegetation. They noticed a small group of men riding toward them.

As the group got close enough they recognized Sheriff Treadwell riding in the lead.

This is bad, Bryan thought, *really bad.*

"Well, look what we have here, boys," Treadwell said. "Good things happen if you're just patient."

They pulled up all around the wagon. Treadwell rode up next to them. Judge O'Dell rode up to the other.

"Guess you kids will be going back with us, now that you ain't got your ranger protecting you no more," the sheriff said.

"He said if you did this that he'd come after you."

Treadwell laughed, "He was just blowing smoke. We all know that."

"What's the charge?"

"The young lady there has to complete her trip to the orphanage," the judge said in a snippy voice. "The young man will be charged with kidnapping."

"That ain't hardly fair," Bryan growled.

"It's a matter for the court to decide as to what is fair and what isn't," the judge said, "and the court is going to send you to the work farm for a long time. You can be in there with your friend Professor Donovan."

"You have him in jail?" Carol Sue asked.

The judge nodded. "Yes, for aiding and abetting your escape."

The sheriff chuckled. "People have a tendency to not live long enough to get out of the work farm. You're gonna be sorry you set that ranger on me."

Bryan didn't bother to disguise his anger. "You're just being plain spiteful. There's no reason for all this."

Carol Sue added, "It's been weeks, I can't believe you're still pursuing this. He has the legal documentation to show that I'm his ward."

The sheriff grinned. "Papers? I ain't seen no papers."

"Sheriff, this isn't right," Scott yelled.

"You stay out of this."

Bryan thought, *If I let them take me back, we'll never get out of this. There's just one way.*

Sudden as a lightning bolt Bryan leapt from his saddle to land behind the sheriff on his horse. In the same motion he drew his pistol, placing it behind the sheriff's right ear. The entire posse quickly pointed guns at him.

"Oh no, Bryan," Carol Sue screamed.

"Your call, Sheriff," Bryan said. "They shoot me, you don't live long enough to hear me hit the ground."

"You idiots put those guns up," Treadwell yelled.

"No!" Bryan said, "throw 'em down, all the way to the ground, and put those rifles down there with them."

They looked at each other, indecision in their faces. Scott pulled the shotgun from behind the seat. He couldn't cock it and handle it with one hand so he tossed it to Carol Sue. She pulled back the hammers on it. "I'm told I just need to point this in your general direction," she said sweetly.

"You heard her, men," Treadwell said. "I don't think she's kidding."

"You can bet your worthless hide that *I'm* not kidding," Bryan said, "whether she is or not, which I doubt. You've already told me what I have to look forward to. I figure I have nothing to lose."

"You moron," the judge said. "You had to shoot off your big mouth."

Bryan motioned with his gun barrel. "Okay, you in the brown hat. Yes, you. Step down and walk over here." One by one he had the posse dismount and come over where he could cover them while Janet tied their hands behind their back. Once they were all tied, he marched them over to a nearby grove of trees. There he had them sit back-to-back and tied them together in pairs.

"What's this all about?" the judge demanded. "You can't get away with this."

"I think I can. It's like the ranger said, you have no authority over here. I'm going to keep you right where you are until I get a little advice on the subject."

He turned, "Carol Sue, I need you and Janet to take the wagon on in to Shreveport. Send a wire to Davidson and tell him what the situation is. Get back as quick as you can and bring some help if you find someone you can trust."

"Can I trust the law?"

"Normally, I'd say yes. There's no telling how the law might react to these fine citizens though, they might fall for all this stuff they're throwing around. Just follow your instincts."

They stayed just that way, Bryan and Scott baby-sitting the entire group while the ladies ran their errand. In a couple of hours they returned with four men. The men took over the guard detail as Carol Sue explained what had transpired.

"I sent the wire to Davidson in Austin explaining things. He wired right back, and I could tell by the tone of the wire that he was mad. He said he was sending a wire to Turkey Creek informing them that felons have been apprehended by his deputies and that these felons are posing as law officers in direct contradiction to orders from the state of Texas."

"So, we're deputies now?"

"Yes, but listen to this," she said. "The wire said the state of Texas required the material testimony of a witness now in their possession in order to effect their release and that said prisoner was to be sent unescorted immediately as they wished no further difficulty with so called peace officers from outside our jurisdiction."

"And the prisoner is . . . ?"

"The professor."

Bryan slapped his hat on his leg. "That's telling them. Will they do it?"

"What choice do they have?"

"Who are these fellows?"

"Some freight drivers for a Texas freight line. Davidson sent a wire and arranged that too. We're to stay right here and hold these men until Davidson arrives. He said he'd be wearing out horses getting here."

"All the way from Austin?"

"He wasn't in Austin, but apparently Western Union always knows where to reach those guys."

Treadwell spoke up. "That ranger is coming here?"

"That's what he said." She couldn't resist a smile.

"Oh no, I'm dead." Treadwell said, the color draining from his face.

"Oh, I don't think Davidson is the type of man who would do that, but I expect he'll have a few words for you," Bryan said.

He looked around. "I hate to have to mess with it, but I expect we better figure out how to feed these follows."

She waved a hand. "Oh, you don't have to worry about that. The freight line is sending a wagon out with enough food to feed us all. It seems the owner is quite a good friend of Davidson."

"It looks that way. It was a lucky day when we ran into him, wasn't it," she said.

"Don't know what we'd have done if we hadn't."

24

Davidson arrived in two days. Life in the camp had settled into a routine around the makeshift jail that was guarded twenty-four hours a day. More men had arrived from Shreveport attracted by the nature of the project. It had turned into a first class party at the expense of the group from Turkey Creek.

When Davidson rode up, he scarcely wasted time on amenities, but dismounted and strode straight over to the roped enclosure. Treadwell physically cowered.

"Treadwell, I must have not made myself clear about what I'd do if you came after these young people again."

"It wasn't me, the judge ordered me—"

"I'll get around to him in a minute. I didn't give him no orders, but I don't think there should have been any doubt left in your mind as to what I said to you."

"Well I didn't think you meant it literally. I thought—"

Davidson cut him off. "You didn't think at all; that's the problem. For future reference, any time a Texas Ranger tells you anything—anything at all—you can be dead sure he's not just talking to hear his gums flap."

The judge walked over to where the ranger stood. "Now see here, whoever you are, I'm a duly constituted officer of the court and you can't treat me this way. I demand—"

"You're a judge, is that it?"

"Yes."

"Federal?"

"Well, no."

"State? No, it couldn't be state. Indian territory isn't a state. And it can't be county, because there aren't any counties organized over there. Could it be you're a petty *municipal* judge?"

"There's nothing petty about—"

"Everything about you is petty. Everything about this whole deal is petty. So, if you are a *municipal* officer of the court, that would mean your jurisdiction is what?"

"What do you mean?"

"Don't play dumb with me, Judge, although it pains me to use that title on a snake like you. What's your given name?"

"Judge Stanford O'Dell, and I won't tolerate being spoken to in that tone."

"You'll tolerate whatever I tell you to tolerate, Stanford. Now tell me what your official jurisdiction is before I give you some of what I'm about to give Treadwell."

Treadwell backed up three steps. "Give me?"

The judge said tiredly, "My jurisdiction is Turkey Creek."

"Bounded by what?"

"The city limits."

"Are we inside those boundaries at present?"

The judge adopted a haughty look. "You know very well we aren't."

"Don't make me pry this out of you a word at a time, you're making me almighty mad."

"Very well, you're after me to say I'm not within my jurisdiction."

"Now there's a startling revelation. What that means is you're over in my jurisdiction posing as a peace officer."

"We are duly constituted—"

Davidson continued to cut him off, a sign his patience was wearing thin.

"Yeah, you said that, but you aren't duly constituted in Texas, so here you are breaking the law. That's an offense I could lock you up for a tolerable amount of time over."

"You can't—"

"Go sit down, Stanford, before you make me any madder than you already have. If you stay quiet as a mouse between now and when I get around to dealing with you, you may get to go home someday."

The little man returned to where he had been sitting. His demeanor clearly said he had been solidly put in his place.

Davidson started peeling his hat and his guns off. "Treadwell, peel that gun belt off and get out here."

"It's Sheriff Tre—"

"You'll never hear me put that title in connection with your name. No kind of sheriff I ever ran into would let himself be a party to these kind of shenanigans. If I have to come in there after you, I most sincerely guarantee you'll regret it."

Treadwell tossed his hat and gun belt to one of his men. "All right, let's get this over with."

"What?" Davidson said, "no threats, no bravado, not even going to threaten me with a licking?"

"I'm under no illusions about going up against you."

"A big man like you? You ain't much good unless you're throwing your weight around against a couple of young people, are you? Only when you tried that Bryan put you and your whole posse right up a tree, didn't he?"

"There's just no reason for us to—"

"Still hoping to talk your way out of it, aren't you?" Davidson swung suddenly, connecting with Treadwell's jaw. The sheriff went down like a sack of grain dropped off the back of a wagon.

"That was impressive," the ranger said.

"I've had enough."

"One punch and you're down for the count? I don't think so. You can stand up on your hind legs and give an account of yourself like you were actually a man, or I can get down there on your chest and sit on it while I beat your face into ground meat. Your choice."

Treadwell made no move to get up.

"I figure that's half of your voting population over there in that jail, and I'm guessing your next election is going down the drain even as we speak."

Treadwell got to his feet reluctantly.

Davidson said, "I'll tell you what, you big sack of cow dung, the better account you give of yourself the less I'm gonna hurt you. You just keep whining and covering up and I'm gonna beat you beyond recognition."

Treadwell sighed and turned loose a punch. Davidson blocked it aside as if swatting a fly.

"My mother once slapped me harder than that. Let's see what you've got."

"You . . . you . . ." Treadwell waded in, throwing punches with both hands. The ranger caught them easily. The sheriff tried to kick Davidson and he blocked the kick with his knee, again throwing a huge punch that sent Treadwell sprawling.

"Well, make the man mad, and he at least gives it a try. My Aunt Suzie could take you without having to take her apron off, but at least you made some sort of effort. Now get up."

"I can't."

"You better, or it's whupping time, with me sitting on your chest. You better get up and get it on, or they're gonna have to take you home in a sack."

Treadwell came off the ground with a roar, catching the ranger around the waist, carrying him back against a tree. He swung several punches with all his strength hitting Davidson in the midsection. The ranger grunted once, then spun Treadwell around, pinning him against the tree. He slapped him, openhanded, back and forth several times, then came with a punch from down low, sweeping up, catching Treadwell under the jaw, snapping his head back against the tree. The big man slumped to the ground and didn't move.

Davidson walked over to the enclosure. "We got anybody else who still fancies themselves a peace officer? I got it in me to take you all one at a time and give you some of the same."

"Not if it means fighting you," somebody said. "I don't want out that bad."

"Okay, everybody but Stanford and Treadwell can collect your things and go. I want you out of Texas as fast as your horses will get you there, and I don't want to ever see you back here again. I don't want any misunderstanding about this. If either of these young people have any more problem with a single one of you, even if they come back to Turkey Creek and knock on the door of your house, I'm going to come boiling up there and knock heads together until there isn't an unscrambled brain in town. Is that clear?"

There was a chorus of grumbling assent. This was a band of believers now.

"One more thing. If you people have any pride at all, now that you've seen the color of the backbones on these two men, you'll see to it that there's a new judge and a new sheriff by the time they get back home—if they ever do."

The men looked at each other. One said, "Funny thing, Ranger, we've already been talking about doing just that very thing."

"I'm glad to hear that. Now git!"

There was a scurry as men gathered their things, saddled, and mounted as if the devil himself were after them. The judge said, "This is preposterous. You're letting them go and keeping us?"

"They were only riding along with you. They thought you were really somebody. You two are the ones I'm holding accountable for all this. You ain't going nowhere until the professor gets here. I'll decide what to do with you then."

He looked at the heap over to the side. "And when Treadwell wakes up, you make sure he hears every bit of what I just said."

He turned to walk away, but stopped and turned back. "I'll tell you one more thing. I figure those men will be telling the straight of it. I wouldn't give a hoot for your chances of keeping them jobs you're so proud of when they get through telling folks what's been happening. If I were you, I wouldn't even go back. But the same thing I told them goes double for you. If I let you go, and that's a pretty tall *if,* the mood I'm in now, you ain't welcome in Texas, not now . . . not ever."

25

As it happened with the first time they ever saw him, they heard the professor long before he came into view. They rushed out to meet him.

"Professor, are you all right?"

"Thanks to you."

"Thanks to your ranger friend."

Bryan made the introductions. "Professor Harold Donovan, this is Texas Ranger Clay Davidson."

"I'm indebted to you, sir," the professor extended his hand.

Davidson took it with a smile. "Just doing my job; trying to rid the countryside of venomous snakes. Got a couple of bad ones locked up over there."

The professor walked over to the enclosure. "After the experience I just went through, it does my heart good to see this."

Carol Sue came over to put her arms around him. "I thought if you didn't know where we went, that they couldn't charge you with anything."

"I thought so too, but it didn't work out that way. I'd have done better going with you in the first place."

"I'm just guessing," Davidson said, "but I'd say if that posse hadn't been sidetracked by chasing you down first, that they'd have had all three of you before the day was out. You paid a price for it, but you let these young people get enough of a lead that they could get over here where we could give them a hand."

"I suspect you are only saying that to make me feel less the fool," the professor said, "but should it actually be true, then the price was quite worthwhile."

Bryan put his hand on the old man's shoulder. "They treat you bad?"

"The conditions were deplorable, the food was atrocious, the company I was subjected to was outlandish, but other than that it was only terrible."

Bryan looked at the ranger. "I intended to try and buy myself a dictionary while I was in Ft. Worth so I could understand what he talks about, but I forgot to do it."

Davidson laughed. "He does use a mouthful of words, all right. Well, Professor, you're here to testify at a trial, to determine whether these rascals get to go home or not."

"If it is up to me, I have to tell you I find revenge is a dish that is always served cold and contains little nutrition."

"I don't follow you," Davidson said.

The professor looked at Treadwell, who had just sat up and was trying to clear his head. "What happened to the sheriff? He looks a bit used."

"Some people don't take instruction well," Davidson said with a crooked grin. "They have to get educated the hard way."

"You don't say. Well, if there is anything you require that I learn, just speak right up. I assure you I'll assimilate the information much more readily than he apparently did."

The professor got a blank look on his face, "Where was I? Oh yes, if you require that I testify in order to try them for jurisdictional difficulties, I shall be happy to do my civic duty. However, if the purpose is to exact some measure of retribution for their treatment of me, it isn't necessary. I am a most forgiving man. Time and energy wasted on hatred and ill will is time truly and irretrievably squandered."

"I admire your ability to do that. I'm not sure I could be that forgiving," Davidson said.

"I can't say I am always completely successful with such a degree of forbearance, but I certainly am inclined to try."

"You guys hear that?" Davidson walked over to confront his remaining two prisoners. "You people treated him like dirt, and he wants to live and let live. He's a far better man than you miserable critters are. You don't deserve it, but I'm going to honor his request."

Treadwell had gotten to his feet. He seemed to be having trouble focusing.

"Treadwell, did *Stanford* here tell you the rules of this here game?"

The judge seemed poised to object to the intentional use of his first name, but apparently thought better of it. "He's just now come around."

"Well, let me do the honors then. Thanks to the professor, I'm gonna let you go. I want you out of Texas as fast as your horses can carry you without doing them harm. I expect your entire community to leave these three people alone the rest of your and their natural lives, even should they happen to physically show up in your town again, though I can't imagine why they'd want to. I'll add one further condition in your honor, Treadwell. You bring shame to the entire profession of being a peace officer. I'm going to ride into Turkey Creek some day when you least expect it. If I find you wearing that badge, I'm going to rip it off you, then I'm going to finish the licking I gave you a small taste of. You didn't seem to understand what I told you last time. Are you completely clear on what I'm saying now?"

"It isn't fair."

"Nobody ever said life had to be fair. You answer my question or I won't wait until I come up there to further your education."

"I understand. I don't think I'm going back to Turkey Creek anyway."

"Then I suggest you go east, Treadwell. You aren't cut out to be a western man. And you oughta take this pitiful excuse for a judge with you. He isn't either."

"I have too much in Turkey Creek to walk away from," the judge objected.

"Then go pick it up. I figure the town isn't going to have much use for you regardless what you decide."

"You say we have no authority over here," the judge said. "The same goes for you over there."

"I don't need any authority for what I have in mind. If you think that title you value so highly will protect you from getting some of what Treadwell got, you best give it another thought. You better heed what I say. I'm not going to be so gentle the next time we meet."

"If I'm free to go, I for one am ready to get on my horse and take your advice to the letter," Treadwell said.

"Treadwell, you can't get out of my sight fast enough to suit me."

Bryan introduced the professor to Scott and Janet.

"I'm pleased to meet you," he said, "and my thanks to you for what you have done for my young friends."

"They've done much more for us than we have for them."

"Well, be that as it may, it appears our little enterprise has its first employees."

The professor had been sorely used. That was evident as they began treating scrapes, lash marks, and abrasions after he took a creek bath.

"They used us as hard labor," he said with a wan smile.

He held out his hands for inspection. "That's something I've always tried to avoid in my life."

Carol Sue gently applied some of the professor's own ointment, rubbing it in slowly and gently as he talked. "We were surface mining, and the guards drove us hard. If you fell, they beat you until you got up . . . or died."

Bryan scowled, "I can't believe they do that in the name of the law."

"I think they contract out for private enterprise to run the establishment. They incarcerate and care for the prisoners in return for the labor for their various operations. The government is spared the bother and the expense. I've long been a proponent of free enterprise, but in this case . . ."

"Just terrible," Carol Sue said.

Bryan shook his head sadly. "I'm sure sorry we got you into it."

"Ah, but you didn't get me into it, my young friend. It was my own failure to control my wagging tongue that was my downfall. Had I not baited that curmudgeon from the orphanage, I should have never run afoul of the law, nor would you have gotten in their ill-favor. Had I shown enough foresight to curtail my tongue and we had simply thanked him and walked out quietly, we could have merely proceeded on our way. OW!"

"I'm sorry," Carol Sue said gently, "that one is pretty sore, I take it?"

"I hurt in places I didn't even know I had. However, I am probably in better shape physically than I have ever been. The exercise program I always said I would do someday, to prevent myself from going to seed, was forced upon me."

Carol Sue finished and helped him put his shirt back on.

"But enough lamenting and feeling sorry for myself," the professor said cheerily. "We are at the dawn of a new day and quite literally so. I think another change in my nature has come of this. I no longer feel the wanderlust that has plagued me all my life. I feel the need to settle down and to plant some roots. I harbor an insane desire to spend time in a rocking chair on a shady porch. I suppose I must admit I'm getting old."

"You're going to give up your business?" Bryan asked.

"Of course not. I have in mind a substantial expansion. Instead of making such small amounts as I travel around the country, I'm thinking about a central manufacturing point. I'm thinking about a distribution chain with employees. I envision hiring some salesmen to go work our territory for us. I see delivery wagons going out delivering the product and returning with raw products for our manufacturing."

"Whew," Bryan said. "I never imagined."

"Wow," Scott said, "looks like I hooked my wagon to a shooting star."

"You did indeed, my friend," the professor patted Scott on the shoulder, making sure it was his good shoulder. "At last I shall put my formal training to use. And the investment of these two young people made it possible. It provided a big enough seed to get it underway. It will be half yours, and you shall help me build it."

"It takes my breath away," Carol Sue said.

Bryan added, "Some people asked me if they could invest."

"And they can." The professor was getting excited. "We shall sell stock. I know others who will buy in."

"This is exciting," Carol Sue's eyes were dancing. "We're going into business."

"We've been in business; you are in on the birth of an industry. Why, before we're through we'll be nationwide."

"Is there a particular place we need to go to set it up?" Bryan asked.

"Since we will be bringing raw product in to a central point and doing all of the processing there, I would think we could set up anywhere. You have a place in mind?"

"Yes," Carol Sue said. "The people at Clarendon were so wonderful to us. They wanted us to come back and settle there. We sure did like it there."

"I've been there. Did some business with a Mr. Rosenfeld at the general store, as I recall. Yes, I liked it very much."

"Uh, wait a minute. They aren't likely to take well to your setting up a still there. There is no alcohol allowed there," Bryan said.

"I don't think it'll be a problem in the least. We just need to let them know right up front that it is for medicinal purposes only and that none will be sold for recreational consumption. Leave it to me. I'll make them see we will be bringing prosperity to the community and jobs, diversifying their economy. Trust me, the city fathers will love it."

Carol Sue spoke quietly to the professor. "Are you sure, Professor? Are you sure you are ready to leave the road?"

"Yes, my dear, I am. The wanderlust is gone. I felt it leave as surely as the casting out of a demon. Now I feel the need to build, to forge an organization that will help people all over."

He walked over and put his hands on each of their shoulders. "And it's because of the two of you. You make me feel young again. Now gather up and let's head back to that city you love so much."